'Oh, no, you don't!' His eyes were twinkling. 'I expect at least the semblance of gracious defeat. Now, admit you were wrong. . .'

Caroline felt her arms tingle in the warmth of his grasp and she leaned slightly backwards, feeling flustered. Did he expect her to arm wrestle with him? She laughed to cover her confusion. 'All right, you win. I was wrong.'

'Good girl. Now. . .what do I win?' David's grin was teasing. His hands had slid down her arms and were imprisoning her hands.

'I. . .I didn't know there was a p. . .prize.' Caroline felt her breathing oddly constricted by a sudden jolt of her heart. His nearness seemed to make her senses whirl and she resisted an impulse to bury her head against that familiar shoulder and have his arms enclose her again.

DELICATE HARMONY

BY
ELIZABETH FULTON

MILLS & BOON LIMITED
ETON HOUSE   18–24 PARADISE ROAD
RICHMOND   SURREY   TW9 1SR

First published in Great Britain 1990
by Mills & Boon Limited

© Elizabeth Fulton 1990

Australian copyright 1990
Philippine copyright 1990
This edition 1990

ISBN 0 263 76887 2

Set in 10 on 10 pt Linotron Plantin
03-9007-63374
Typeset in Great Britain by Centracet, Cambridge
Made and printed in Great Britain

CHAPTER ONE

'YOU never!' A stifled giggle accompanied this exclamation directed towards the slim back of Nurse Caroline Lawson who was concentrating on tying her long jet-black hair into a Grecian knot on the top of her head.

'Well, not exactly.' Caroline turned from the mirror and smiled at her wide-eyed classmate. 'I just whispered under my breath. I don't think the senior tutor heard me. I certainly hope she didn't! I don't want to be disciplined before we've really started here.' She picked up the navy-blue cardigan from her bed and wrapped it around her shoulders. 'Sometimes I wish we wore uniforms during our RMN training. Cloaks would be of more use than my threadbare woollies. Come on, Tracey, we'll be late.'

Tracey Wilmer reluctantly rolled herself up from the deep armchair in the corner of the small room. 'Why you always have to be early to lectures, I'll never know. You've never been late yet!'

'Just neurotic, I guess.' Caroline grinned at her friend. 'At least we can get seats in the back, if we're early. Then maybe no one will notice us and ask questions. I haven't had time to read up the chapter for today's lecture yet.'

She cheerfully pushed Tracey ahead of her and turned to lock the door behind them. The nurses' residence was always security-conscious after unknown intruders had made off with a sister's cherished heirloom clock and one of the students had lost a wallet.

The two girls made their way down the long corridor and reached the outside door without meeting any other residents. The different shifts and timetables made it unusual for the building to appear fully occupied, although every room was taken by students and staff working in the large psychiatric hospital.

'Oh, lordy be.' Tracey gulped as they pushed the door

against the brisk January wind and prepared to make a dash across the bare lawn to the opposite building. 'You'd think they'd build underground tunnels or something. Country living in the depths of England is only for the hardy!'

They huddled in their light cardigans and ran quickly, reaching the School of Nursing building slightly out of breath.

'Oh, Tracey. . .' Caroline let out a soft wail as she stopped short. 'I forgot my notes from yesterday. I'll have to go back.'

'Why bother? You'll remember the details. You always do. I'll lend you some paper if you need it.'

They had halted just inside the door, which was abruptly pushed open behind them, sending both girls suddenly back against the wall.

'Here, watch it——' Tracey's indignant yelp was cut off abruptly as they both looked up at the tall figure who had entered so quickly in a burst of fresh, cool air.

'Whoops, sorry. Hello there.' A pair of twinkling blue eyes looked down at both flushed faces. 'Anyone know where the lecture on "Historical Aspects of Schizophrenia" is supposed to be?'

For some unaccountable reason Caroline felt her already flushed cheeks deepen. The clear blue eyes sparkling down at her belonged to the clean-cut features of Dr David Hunter. It would be difficult not to recognise him, she thought. Few psychiatric senior registrars walked around in the middle of an English winter sporting a deep tan.

He looked as if he had just stepped off the ski slopes, which was quite probable; she had heard that the Adonis of Castleview Hospital took leaves of absence whenever the sporting scene beckoned. They had never met, but Caroline had noted the blond, tanned man in the general rounds.

As Tracey stuttered out directions to the lecture-room, Caroline surreptitiously watched Dr Hunter's face. A sense of barely controlled vitality seemed to surround the man. Up close, his jawline wasn't quite as square as she had thought, and his nose was very nice and straight.

His mouth was. . .well, it was really quite a lovely mouth, especially when he was smiling, the way he was smiling now. . .

She jerked back from her tumbling thoughts as she found herself being scrutinised by those deep blue eyes. She blinked up at him. Suddenly those smiling eyes held a quite extraordinary glow that seemed to see right through her and she trembled slightly.

Caroline backed away and felt the reassuring solidity of the wall behind her. She was aware of her discomfort and shook herself mentally, forcing a cool smile.

'And are you lovely ladies attending the lecture?' The warmth of his smile was echoed in his voice, as he looked at Caroline. If he noticed her slight shrinking away, he gave no sign.

'Yes, it's part of our course, Dr Hunter,' Caroline answered quietly. She was surprised that the tumult of feelings his closeness had provoked did not affect her voice. Praise be for professionalism, she thought.

'Students, then? But I think not student nurses?' He sounded genuinely interested in placing them within the professional heirarchy. Neither nurse was wearing a name badge.

'We're both graduate nurses—doing the RMN specialist course.' Tracey seemed quite at ease with the handsome doctor and Caroline recognised the cheerful flirtatious tone of her friend. She smiled more easily. Tracey could always be relied on to lighten up an atmosphere. Laughter and cheerful chatter came so readily to her friend; Caroline often wondered why the two of them should get along so well—being so different.

David Hunter's open friendly smile included both nurses. 'Good, I'll look forward to your contributions.' With this, he was away down the corridor, with his hands shoved in his jacket pockets and walking with energetic jaunty steps.

Caroline moved away to slowly follow the direction taken by Dr Hunter.

They reached the small seminar-room and Caroline was glad to see that there were still two seats in the back corner. During the last four weeks of the introductory

block it seemed the others had become accustomed to
leaving the seats vacant for the two of them.

Caroline noted that most of the fifteen students in
their set had developed the habit of going to the same
seats each day. Human behaviour is very strange, she
thought. But then, that was what doing an RMN was all
about. That was why she was here. She wondered if she
would ever be able to learn enough to help the emotionally ill; there seemed to be so much she didn't
understand.

As she settled into her usual seat by the back corner
near the window, Caroline watched her classmates casually. A sudden hush descended on the room, and,
without looking up, Caroline knew that their lecturer
had arrived. She kept her eyes firmly on the page in
front of her as a warm, cheerful voice began the lecture.
The material was new to her, and she found that she
wanted to make good notes and began to concentrate on
what Dr Hunter was saying. He was outlining the history
of schizophrenia and her pen began to move rapidly
across the page. She had always been lucky enough to be
able to listen and write at the same time. It helped if the
person talking was fairly well organised, and she had to
admit that Dr Hunter seemed to have his material in
good order.

Just as she was beginning to understand the form of
his ideas—the change from regarding delusional behaviour as possession by the devil or evil forces to a
therapeutic approach developed after a French doctor
freed the inmates of an asylum in Paris—Caroline heard
Annabelle's voice from the front row interrupting with a
question.

Caroline frowned slightly. Trust Annabelle, she always
had to be noticed. Just when the story was getting
interesting, too. She put down her pen and watched Dr
Hunter. That certainly was not difficult; he was very
pleasant to look at. Caroline frowned at herself. The
doctor seemed to be enjoying the attention of his eager
listener and Caroline watched, surprised at her own
feelings of disapproval, as David Hunter grinned widely
at Annabelle. He was flirting with her! Just his type,

thought Caroline. Fluff and nonsense. Well, no, that was unfair. Annabelle was a perfectly nice girl, as Aunt Betty would probably say.

Caroline allowed her mind to drift slightly. She wondered what Aunt Betty would make of David Hunter. Too handsome by half, she would say. Handsome is as handsome does. Dear Aunt Betty. Caroline felt her eyes moisten. She missed Aunt Betty, homespun proverbs and all. She blinked quickly and brought her attention back to the classroom.

Annabelle and David Hunter were laughing! Caroline looked over quickly at Miss Mansin. The senior tutor was smiling benignly at her guest lecturer.

Caroline was startled to hear her name and she looked up at the front of the room.

'Nurse Lawson, is it?' Dr Hunter was smiling broadly in her direction. He had a named seating plan on the lectern in front of him. Miss Mansin must have noted where they all sat. Caroline's heart sank. She always hated being called on in a group.

She nodded, mutely, waiting for his inevitable question. She prayed silently that she could remember whatever it was he would want to know.

'Why do you think that delusional people were put in dungeons?' His tone was light and friendly. Caroline thought the content of his question and his manner seemed strange opposites. Jail was hardly an amusing matter.

She thought before she spoke. 'There was probably nowhere else.'

David Hunter nodded. 'Perhaps. Can you think of what it must have been like when Pinel struck off their chains and brought them out?'

'The light must have hurt their eyes.' Her answer was spontaneous, without her thinking, and she blushed to hear giggles from the group. She could hear Annabelle's laughter but she kept her eyes resolutely forward, answering David Hunter's look without blinking or turning away. Her fingers tightened on the pen and she swallowed quickly, to ease the tightness in her throat.

He gave her a quizzical smile, with an oddly gentle

twist to his firm mouth. 'Yes, I'm sure it did. I hadn't thought of that.' He leaned forward slightly, balancing his broad shoulders on his elbows at the edges of the lectern. 'What I was thinking of was—what would it have been like for the people of Paris?'

He was watching her face with intent interest. This slim, elegant nurse who hid at the back of the room had an appealing stillness. He was finding it difficult to remember why it was he had called on her in the first place. Her answer had moved him deeply. She had shown an instinctive insight into the feelings of those long-ago patients and he felt slightly ashamed that he had inadvertently exposed her to the laughter of the group.

Caroline was answering his question. 'They might have been angry, or afraid. I don't know really. . .' Her voice trailed off into uncertainty. He was asking her for opinions, not facts, and she could never be certain what opinions people wanted from her. Facts were much easier. She could remember facts but opinions were sometimes too personal.

As if aware of her discomfort, David Hunter drew back and, placing one hand in his jacket pocket, angled away from her to face the opposite side of the room. 'Indeed, the good citizens of Paris were very unhappy with Pinel. They thought he should be locked up, along with his demented prisoners!' The light laughter from the group now seemed appropriate and Caroline relaxed.

The lecture continued with no more interruptions and David Hunter did not call on any other students, nor did he look towards the corner again. When Miss Mansin rose to thank him, he nodded with his ever-ready grin and noted it had indeed been his pleasure.

After he had left the room at his usual energetic speed, the student group exploded into giggles and chatter. The talking stilled as Miss Mansin rose and placed some papers on the lectern.

'Dr Hunter always ends our introductory block on an upbeat note.' She pulled the top paper from her pile, 'However, to get back to details of today's world—this is a list of the ward assignments for next week. As you know from the course outline, this placement will last eight weeks.'

The group of students immediately gave her their total attention. Although they had toured the wards earlier, actually joining the working staff was a more serious matter. The atmosphere was tight with expectation and tension. They had all heard from student gossip which wards were more desirable and waited to hear their individual fates for the next two months.

'Before reading the list, I would like to remind you of our expectations.' The senior tutor watched the intent faces in front of her. 'In this group you are all state registered nurses, or RGNs as I must learn to say.' She smiled briefly. 'We all become accustomed to familiar habits, but I will try to adapt to changing times.

'Because you are all trained nurses,' she continued, 'more will be expected from you than some students who are still doing the basic RMN training.' She paused. 'Although no one will expect a high degree of clinical psychiatric knowledge from you,' a few faint self-conscious titters greeted this statement, 'we do expect common sense and an understanding of professional nursing behaviour.

'The patients here are still patients and require the same level of professional service you have learned in the general field of medicine. The expertise will come later.' She nodded quietly at the serious young faces. 'That skill can take years to acquire and we are all still learning.'

She smiled broadly at them. 'I hope you enjoy your learning on the wards and wish you all the best. There will be clinical instructors on each unit, of course, but you will also be answerable to the sisters and charge nurses. They will all be happy to have you. You are very much needed.'

Lowering her half-moon spectacles to read her papers, Miss Mansin then began to read the assignment list.

Caroline heard her name linked to Folkestone Ward. Male admissions. Her heart sank. She had been hoping for a female ward; women were always easier to talk to. And admissions would probably be unpredictable. Until patients were diagnosed, how could they be treated properly?

Her mood remained thoughtful as the group disbanded in a soft flutter of quiet talk, comparing assignments when out of earshot of the senior tutor.

Caroline frowned slightly. It did seem inappropriate to take the subject of psychiatry as lightly as Dr Hunter had appeared to. Even if his face looked so alive when he smiled, with all the little laugh lines crinkling up the edges of those deep blue eyes. His eyes seemed to change colour, she thought. Sometimes they were light and clear, sometimes dark and intense.

Silly! She shrugged off such adolescent thinking. It didn't matter if he had pink-striped eyes; he was nothing to her. She was here to learn and that was all that mattered.

She followed her friend into the small kitchen on the ground floor of the residence.

Tracey was reading the tattered notices. 'Hey, look at this. There's a Welsh night tomorrow at the local pub. At least, I think it's a pub—the Good Neighbour. Anyone been there yet?'

'Yes, I went last week. It's a sort of dining place with a bar at the front. Service was terrible.' This came from the reclining Alison.

Tracey turned to Caroline. 'What about it? One last fling before the gates close behind us. We might even meet some locals; this is stockbroker commuter country, after all!' She grinned mischievously. 'There might even be a sing-song for you!'

Caroline, curled up in an overstuffed chair, blushed slightly. Her habit of singing in the bath had been the subject of much teasing from her new friends. 'I don't know, Tracey. I wanted to visit the village shops tomorrow and catch up on some reading.'

'Oh, no, you don't!' This exclamation came from Beth. 'You may be the clever Dick in this set, but a class swot we will not allow!' A loose cushion was tossed lightly on to Caroline's lap.

Sheltering behind her upraised notebook, Caroline cheerfully ducked the assault and threw the pillow back

at Beth. She was then forced to leap up, dropping her
book, to run behind Alison's sofa to avoid the brandished
pillow being re-aimed at her head.

'You missed her, you twit!' Alison had grabbed
another loose pillow and joined the fray, heaving a
cushion at Beth who had rapidly taken refuge behind the
open door. Alison's missile landed softly on the sandy-
coloured head of a young man who had just appeared at
the edge of the doorway.

'Oh, Andrew, I am sorry, but it's Caroline's fault.
She's trying to avoid her social obligation to uphold our
set's mental health.' Alison did not sound very repentant.

Andrew sat comfortably on the floor and leaned against
a low table as he looked up at Caroline. 'It would do us
all good to get out—help with the collywobbles before
next week.'

'Are you nervous, too?' Caroline had curled up on the
edge of Alison's settee. 'I don't know why I am. Something new, I guess.'

'Sure. It's hard to go back to being a student again.'
Andrew had been a staff nurse in Paediatrics for several
years and the girls nodded at him with understanding.

Andrew left them to find Tom and inform him of the
plans for Saturday. Caroline slipped away to return to
her room. She had mixed feelings about the proposed
expedition but couldn't really understand her own unsettled mind.

Starting something new and challenging in an unfamiliar environment was not usually a difficulty. She knew
she had the ability to learn as she had always been a good
student. She had loved her contact with psychiatric
patients during her basic nurse training. Still, she had an
uneasiness that she couldn't explain.

She turned her attention to her notes from Dr
Hunter's lecture. They were clear and well organised;
she had to admit that he had been easy to follow. She
read over the basic history of psychiatry he had outlined.
Such people had always been viewed as outsiders in any
society and it seemed that not much had changed since
the days of the witch hunts. Reading the words, she
could hear his voice in her head. He had a strong,

forceful voice, she remembered. The sort of voice that made you want to listen to him talk, regardless of what he might say.

She blushed with the memory of her silly answer in class. Still, Dr Hunter hadn't laughed. Caroline sighed and closed her notebook. Enough of such thinking. She could do some reading tomorrow morning and review the basic diagnostic terminology on Sunday afternoon. With these firm resolutions she went to find Tracey to go over to the staff canteen for tea.

As she surveyed the results of her efforts the following evening, Caroline felt reasonably satisfied. She moved experimentally sideways and was pleased with the soft lines of her fawn-coloured mohair jumper that allowed glimpses of snowy white frilled collar and cuffs at the edges of the round neck and full sleeves. It was warm and cosy, as was her favourite chocolate-brown woollen skirt.

She smiled—not as seductive as Annabelle's choice of clothing would be, but much more comfortable. Her eyes moved up to the red scarf she had tied around her long hair, held up high on the crown of her head and allowed to flow loosely in a thick shining mane past her shoulders.

She had to admit that the glimpses of scarlet silk beneath the gleaming darkness added a touch of life. Aunt Betty had always called her 'my little princess Persephone'; perhaps tonight she would have approved. Caroline had a brief instant of wishing her aunt were here to fuss a bit over her. She brushed away the slight pang of loss and leaned over closer towards the old mirror above the bureau.

Were her eyes darker or was it just a distortion? Perhaps the gold earrings picked up a glow she hadn't noticed before. No matter. She would probably have dark rings under her eyes tomorrow if she stayed up too late tonight. She wrinkled her nose at her reflection. She did wish her face weren't so obviously heart-shaped. There certainly was no elegant bone-structure in the face staring back at her so quizzically—merely rounded smooth cheeks reflecting the pale golden glow of the glistening ear-drops.

Caroline started to hum a tune to herself. She wondered what a 'Welsh night' would turn out to be. Surely there would be music—weren't the Welsh all singers? She began to sing a bit louder and swayed slowly to her own invented melody. It had been a long time since she had listened to live music, and how much she had missed it.

Inventing a counterpoint harmony for herself, she wondered idly if she might be able to find a piano somewhere around the hospital. She knew there wasn't one in the residence, having already searched in all the public rooms. Her fingers itched to play again and she stretched her fingers and hands in flickering arpeggios in the air.

A laughing voice from the open door put an end to her dreaming. 'Not bad—not bad at all!'

Caroline turned to smile and shrug at Tracey's approval.

'Andrew is shouting outside, swearing he'll never do chauffeur duty for us again if we don't hurry.'

'Coming.' Caroline quickly slipped into her old warm quilted jacket, pushed a wallet into a large pocket and, taking time only to quickly lock her door, dashed after the disappearing Tracey.

The two girls clambered into the back of the borrowed square-set vehicle.

'Apologies, ladies,' Andrew grunted slightly as he manipulated the steering-wheel, 'I'm not used to driving mini tanks with six gears.'

'Well, watch you don't demolish the lodge house.' Tracey giggled. 'Poor old Charlie would have a coronary on the spot.'

'Not likely. He'd probably never notice,' answered Tom. 'Oblivious to everything outside his racing form is old Charlie. Plus whatever's in that flask of his!'

The group laughed, then waved at the porter in the lit window of the gatekeeper's small cottage. True to Tom's prediction, the bent head visible beside the frayed curtain did not look up or acknowledge their departure.

'Why do they bother with a porter anyway? They never lock the gates.' Beth's voice sounded muffled from beneath Tracey's shoulder.

'Another relic of the Dark Ages. Apparently you used to have to sign in and out every night and they locked everything up at ten or something.' Andrew was concentrating on his braking as they neared the roundabout to turn into the village road.

'He's probably been there so long, everyone's forgotten about him—like woodworm. . .oh, watch out, Andrew, you nearly hit that rabbit!' Annabelle squealed suddenly.

'As a city lad, I'm not too accustomed to rabbits on the road. Well, here we are.' He sighed with relief as they pulled into the brightly lit courtyard of the restaurant.

As they climbed out, the nature of the 'Welsh night' became apparent. The rousing voices of male singing reached them through the open door.

Caroline exclaimed with pleasure, 'They sound very good!' She hurried to the door without waiting for the others. The voices *were* good and she could hear a fine strong tenor in the group, carrying the high descant with ease.

As she entered the doorway, she stood transfixed, aware of nothing but the sight and sound of the singers across the room. A group of casually dressed men were leaning against the bar, singing with joyous abandon. The central figure was the tenor, towering over the others, with his fair hair shining in the mirrored reflection of the ceiling lights. His head was thrown back and his voice was soaring up to the rafters.

Shivers of exquisite pleasure shot through Caroline as the magnificent sound reached through her heart to the depths of her being. Through a sudden mistiness in her eyes she recognised with a shock that the creator of such powerful beauty was none other than Dr David Hunter.

CHAPTER TWO

As SHE stood stock still and allowed the richness of the music wash over her, Caroline became aware that a subtle change in the timbre of the tenor's singing had caused the others to fall silent. She listened with growing wonder at the full-throated sound, as he modulated each note with caressing warmth and care. The singer seemed oblivious to all around him. The lilting melody became a tender lullaby, grew to a yearning lament and then changed to a sweet poignancy with the final note fading upwards as ethereal as a prayer.

His final lingering note hung in the silence for a few seconds before the crowded room erupted in a roar of clapping and whistling. David Hunter blinked his eyes, then turned with a laugh to his companions.

'Drinks on me, lads. Singing is thirsty work!' He pulled a few pound coins from his zippered jacket and placed them before a smiling barman. 'Put the rest on tick, will you, Tim?'

'Aye, Doctor. Have one on the house. It's not often we hear the old songs sung like that.' He had started pulling the pints for the jostling drinkers.

David Hunter smiled and shrugged with slight embarrassment before turning to scan the bar-room. Caroline had been wrong to think he had been unaware of his surroundings. Out of the corner of his eye he had seen her enter and stop abruptly. He had been acutely aware of her concentrated quietness and for some inexplicable reason he had felt the need to reach with his voice through to the heart of that stillness.

As he had expanded deep within himself for the necessary breath, he had sensed a power he had not known for years. The sounds had deepened as his throat had opened to release a forgotten strength. He had sung for the listener standing immobile by the door, exulting in his rediscovered control, weaving each note carefully into an intricate pattern.

The sudden crash of applause had startled him and now he looked around for that one important listener. She wasn't there. Using his considerable height to advantage, he slowly searched the room. Surely that red scarf tied on a shining black head would not be too difficult to find. He moved slowly through the bar-room, nodding at familiar faces and easily accepting compliments from the regulars. As he reached the door to the dining area he smiled softly. On the edge of a group at a corner table his eye lit on a bent dark head. Rich scarlet folds lay across a gently curved cheek, with semi-hidden twinkling gold glints catching the light.

'Good evening, all.' His voice was light and cheerful. He glanced down at all the group, noting Caroline Lawson's still lowered head. Did the brief menu really demand such uninterrupted concentration? He smiled broadly. 'I see you've discovered the local hostelry. Not much but all we have, I'm afraid.'

Caroline glanced briefly up at David Hunter. She was still feeling slightly shaken by the effect his music had had on her and she met a quizzical look.

'Would you like to try the speciality of the house?' He raised his eyebrows slightly.

'That would be fine.' Caroline tried to smile politely, but she could feel her face was stiff.

The other three members of the group echoed their gratitude for his offer. Andrew and Tom were relieved to avoid the necessity of demanding attention in an unfamiliar setting and Beth was delighted at the prospect of simply getting something to eat. This had been beginning to look like a very remote possibility.

'I could use an extra pair of hands, I think.' David Hunter had returned with a tray laden with two steaming bowls. 'It's lamb stew tonight—smells reasonable.'

The aroma was indeed appetising and Beth looked hungrily at the food. Tom laughed, as he and Andrew rose to follow David back to the kitchen. 'Dig in, Beth. We'll bring you back an extra.'

'Do you mind?' Beth didn't want to offend the others, but she was ravenous.

'Go ahead.' Caroline grinned and passed over a large soup spoon. They were all used to Beth's need for sustenance. Tracey was looking hopefully at the second bowl and Caroline pushed it in front of her.

When the men returned, with three more trays, no one appeared to be aware that David Hunter had joined their group. Caroline had certainly noticed the unobtrusive arrival of another chair and was very conscious of the broad shoulder that had settled comfortably beside her.

She kept her head lowered as she ate. It was a good stew and she could understand why the place was crowded. All the hospital staff would be grateful for the chance to taste wholesome food again.

Annabelle was the first to pause in the satisfied munching of fresh vegetables and small chunks of tasty meat. 'Your singing was really good, Dr Hunter.' She gave him a wide smile. 'Where did you learn to sing like that?'

'My misspent youth—as a choirboy. And please, no doctors, just David.' He grinned amicably at the admiring face across the table.

'Oh. . .all right. . . David.' At least she has the grace to colour slightly, thought Caroline as she glanced up at those fluttering eyelashes. Annabelle's questions continued. 'Are you Welsh, then?'

'No, not really. One grandfather was Welsh—he spent his life down the mines. All I inherited was a boy soprano voice, and that was useful enough.' He had returned his attention to his stew and answered her easily.

'Well. . . David. . . I thought it was lovely. Didn't you, Caroline?' She turned her wide eyes over towards Caroline's lowered face. 'Caro sings as well, you know—in the bath!' Her tinkling laugh brought a quiet smile from David and quick kick on the ankle from Tracey.

'Do you?' His quiet voice felt like a whisper on Caroline's cheek.

'Very badly.' At least she didn't have to look at him,

but she raised her head and added, 'It's best if no one can hear me.'

'But wasn't David's singing super?' Annabelle's voice was insistent. Tracey groaned softly.

Caroline felt trapped. What could she say? There were no words to express what she felt. She should be able to toss off a flippant compliment as Annabelle had, but she just couldn't do it. His singing had moved her deeply and she still couldn't understand her own reaction to it.

'There is no need to say anything.' David Hunter spoke quietly, but Caroline could hear the faint echo of disappointment under the friendly tone. Before he could tactfully change the subject, she quickly burst out, 'Yes!'

She glanced up at his face beside her and found the deep blue intensity of his eyes searching her face. There was an odd, indefinable expression on his face and she was reminded of her response to his singing. Caroline returned his gaze solemnly and said simply and softly, 'Thank you.'

An almost imperceptible nod was his response and her heart lifted. He had understood. There was nothing else she need say. She didn't know why she had felt the need to thank him, but anything else would have been wrong. She smiled, grateful of his acceptance of her answer.

The sudden warmth of his expression made her feel slightly uncomfortable and she was relieved when his attention was distracted by a clear voice coming from above their heads.

'David, dear. . .'

The voice belonged to a tall girl who stood tapping an impatient foot beside their table. Caroline's quick side-ways glance caught a glimpse of tousled auburn curls, a pert chin and flashing eyes. She had an impression of blurred, fuzzy edges to the figure before she quickly looked across the table to the others.

As she returned her attention to her bowl, Caroline's ears remained alert.

She noticed David Hunter's voice remained neutral. 'Hello, Henry.' He had put down his spoon quietly when looking up to acknowledge the voice.

Henry? Most Henrys didn't sport a head of carefully

arranged fly-away red hair. Probably short for Henrietta. A bit twee, thought Caroline. Still, it was none of her business.

'David, did you bring the Austin tonight?' The voice was slightly imperious.

'No, just the bike.' His answer remained unruffled, expressing only the mildest curiosity. 'Did you want it?'

'Yes, of course. Rodney has his Porsche and it isn't large enough to carry all of us!' At this statement uttered with a childlike petulance Caroline almost smiled out-right at Tracey's expression. She could read her friend's mind. A Porsche? A man named Rodney? These were high-flyers indeed. She watched Tracey glance over at the far table, undoubtedly wondering which of the laughing young men was the owner of the inadequate automobile.

'Sorry, Henry, I can't help you there. Are you going back to the house?' His tone remained dispassionate in the face of the obvious growing irritation in the girl's manner.

'Well, nothing's happening here—as usual.' The girl's sullenness was very evident and Caroline was reminded of a spoiled child, asking to be continuously amused. She frowned slightly as an unpleasant thought occurred to her. Was Dr David Hunter a member of this Henry's entertainment committee? Or perhaps part of the entertainment?

She swallowed quickly to dislodge the odd lump in her throat and stopped eating abruptly. Suddenly she had had enough of the stew. It seemed to have lost its flavour.

'If you wait a bit, I think Tim has arranged for a local group to play. You might like it.' David Hunter remained seated casually, with his long legs stretched out before him, watching the face above him with a tolerant smile.

'I doubt that. However, it seems there's no help for it.' The gleaming curls were tossed impatiently. 'That moped of yours is absolutely useless. I'll see you later.' A quick flick of a fur-trimmed sleeve accompanied her departure to cross the room back to her lively companions.

Caroline watched the retreating back with a strange sense of discomfort. There had been an aura of ownership in Henry's treatment of David Hunter. He didn't seem the sort of person to be ordered around but he had accepted the girl's behaviour with no apparent discomfiture. Caroline felt confused. There was so much about human behaviour she didn't understand. She was probably guessing wrongly, as usual.

The sudden crash of a drum roll stopped all conversation. All heads turned in the direction of the sound. A space had been cleared near the entrance to the bar-room and a slim young man with a bushy head of blond hair and a wide, engaging grin was seated behind a large set of shiny blue and white drums.

He followed his introductory roll with a staccato rapping, obviously delighted with the crowd's reaction. He tapped out a light rhythm and Caroline let out a soft laugh. He seemed to be speaking to them with his happily beating drumsticks.

David smiled and looked down at her delighted face. 'That's Terry. He's the son of the owner here and he loves drums.'

'He seems to be talking with the beats.' She could not help but admire the boy's instinctive use of the sharp sounds.

'Yes, I think he does. Mind you, he can talk just as much without them—if not more so.' He waved at the boy and received a softly tapped response accompanied by a quick nod and smile. 'He's a smart kid, absolutely mad about drumming.'

As he spoke, the boy Terry was joined by three young men carrying instruments. They settled themselves on chairs in a semi-circle as the bustle in the restaurant quietened in expectation. Caroline noted that the chatter at Henry's table did not lessen and she felt a sense of unease.

She pushed the feeling aside and leaned forward with her elbows on the table. There was to be live music after all, as she had hoped. Regardless of the quality, any music could be enjoyed. The boys had a somewhat battered trombone, a clarinet and a small guitar. Only the drums looked new. She smiled with contentment— the combination might be good.

David Hunter noticed her interest, smiled quietly to himself and leant back with his arm casually laid across the back of Caroline's chair. He had also glanced over at the loudly talking group next to the musicians and he watched them with a thoughtful look in his eye.

As the familiar strains of a currently popular melody started Caroline's fingers automatically fingered an imaginary accompaniment on the table-top. She moved her hands silently and began to tap an unseen foot to the steady rhythm of the soft drumbeat underlying the melody. She became completely absorbed in the sounds and nodded with pleasure as she heard Terry begin improvising. The guitarist, a black lad with a flashing grin, picked it up and the two players wove an intricate counterbeat under the melody carried by the other two.

Two of the young men at the nearby table began to beat time loudly with bangs of cutlery on their table. Caroline's pleasure disappeared as their raucous voices started a chant that sounded rough and aggressive to her ears. She could feel a slight trembling deep within herself. It was an old familiar sensation and she hated it.

She kept her eyes carefully averted from the noisy group of diners and clasped her hands together tightly. Why did she always react this way to any hints of rough behaviour? She had thought she would have outgrown this silly fear by now. She was nearly twenty-one, after all. She wasn't afraid of the dark, or crowds, or heights, or anything else she could think of. She twined her fingers together tightly and took a deep breath. If she couldn't understand her feelings, she would just have to control them.

Suddenly she felt her hands enclosed within a gentle comforting warmth. David Hunter had placed his palm over her knotted fingers and as he lightly deepened his pressure, her eyes flew to his face. She was startled to see a tenderness in the quietly smiling eyes watching her. She flushed and quicky withdrew her hands back to her lap, leaning back from the embarrassment of his touch. How silly he must think she was—a nervous Nellie jumping at every noise.

David had thought nothing of the sort. His gesture had been instinctive and was almost as great a surprise to himself as to Caroline. He had sensed her increasing tension. She reminded him of a tiny bird, alert and tense, waiting to disappear in a flash at the slightest hint of danger. He didn't know what threat she felt, only that he had intended to reassure. His glance at those large, expressive brown eyes had shown him a deep fear that had unsettled him. This girl was very much afraid and aware of her fear, judging from her attempts at control. He wondered if she understood the cause. He certainly didn't—at least not yet.

He looked over at the singing revellers. All off-key, he thought to himself. He kept his arm casually on the table after Caroline withdrew and was aware that she was now seated behind his right shoulder. That's right, little sparrow, you can shelter there. He kept his back between her and the sight of the increasingly belligerent singers and started thinking carefully.

Caroline was grateful for his broad shoulder to hide behind. She knew what he was doing and, strangely, she did feel safer behind the large barrier his back presented. She took several deep breaths and steadied herself slowly. She wished she understood why this happened to her. She didn't mind loud noises. She certainly didn't disapprove of drinking. But somehow the combination made her flutter with fear. Could it be the unpredictability of drunken people? She knew she liked things in order and needed to feel she was in control of her life. Did she really need to feel she was in control of other people? She hoped not—that would be dreadful. She would be a very authoritarian nurse, if that were true.

These thoughts were interrupted as David Hunter turned, smiled quietly and placed his hand briefly on her shoulder. 'Stay here, please.'

As she watched, he rose to saunter across the room and approach the table where the young men were now beginning to spread themselves out into the constricted space between the tables. They were attempting to dance, somewhat unsteadily, to the now barely audible music.

She watched with curiosity as he spoke to the girl Henry, who shrugged and leaned over to one of her loudly singing companions. As some of the party began to struggle to their feet, David disappeared into the barroom, returning in a few moments. Passing the musicians, he winked at the drummer and returned to Caroline's table.

'That lot need a bit more space, so I've suggested they go back to my house. You are all welcome to come, especially if you have transport.' His smile included them all.

Caroline thought she could very well wait, probably indefinitely, to see David Hunter's home, but she had an odd feeling that he had deliberately broken up the noisy party because of her. That idea didn't make sense, but she couldn't quite shake it off. Now that the disruptive diners had been shepherded through the bar, the restaurant had returned to a more pleasant background hum. The music had continued throughout and Caroline looked over at the young drummer.

He caught her glance, grinned and added a few extra whisks on the snare drum. She smiled and nodded a friendly response as she rose to follow the eager steps of Tracey and Annabelle. She turned slightly to wave at Beth and Tom, then turned up the collar of her coat as she met the cold blast of air coming from the opened outside door.

In the lit courtyard David Hunter was directing the dispatch of passengers into cars. The Porsche and the landlord's sedan drove off with a squeal of tyres, leaving two young men leaning heavily against the borrowed Range Rover.

Andrew had come up behind her and muttered, 'I suppose those two lovelies are for me.' He sounded resigned and moved over to open the doors. 'So who's for the motorbike, then?'

Caroline smiled. A large white helmet had been produced and she found it being held out to her.

'Oh. . .just a minute.' She seemed to have no control over events at the moment, but there didn't seem to be time to worry about it. 'I have to take these off. . .' She untied her scarf, took off her earrings and wrapped them carefully into the folded material before putting them into her coat pocket.

'Oh! It's gone!' Her wallet had disappeared. She groaned lightly, 'I'll have to go back. . .'

'What's gone?' David Hunter had watched her preparations with calm patience.

'My wallet. I must have dropped it at the table.' She added, without thinking, 'It has my mad money in it.'

'Mad money?' He sounded curious. 'In that case, it must be retrieved. We can't have mad money running around loose.'

Before she could explain, he had disappeared back into the bar and returned within minutes with her small wallet. 'Tim found this. Is it yours?'

'Yes, thank you.' She replaced it and accepted the helmet without demur. She had already caused enough bother. She sat herself gingerly on the motorcycle and watched with some apprehension as David Hunter adjusted his goggles.

'Now, hang on, please. We'll go slowly so Andrew can follow.' He kicked the starter and the engine responded immediately, sending a shudder through Caroline. She tentatively held on to his jacket with cold fingers.

'No, all the way around, please. I don't want you falling off.' His voice came from over his shoulder.

'I can't get all the way around!' Caroline was exasperated. How was she supposed to hold on the width of him in a leather jacket? There was too much of him and he was too bossy, to boot.

A deep chuckle reached her ears in the depths of the helmet. 'Hang on to my belt, then. Here. . .' He reached behind and put her hands under his jacket on to loops of his wide belt. 'And don't let go.' He slowly moved the cycle out of the courtyard.

Let go? Caroline was clutching his belt for dear life as they swerved carefully into the road leading back to the roundabout. She turned slightly to see the following car.

'Don't turn around, please. You put the balance off.'
The calm voice caused her to mutter slightly but she
turned back and resigned herself to her fate.

She kept her eyes tightly closed until they cornered at
the roundabout. They had turned left on to a country
road and she could smell freshly turned earth on the cold
air. Cautiously opening her eyes, she ventured a peek
around his shoulder. The night seemed very quiet and
wasn't as dark as she had thought. There was clear
moonlight on the road and she could see the grey outlines
of the hedgerows. The quiet, steady motor had a soothing sound and she could feel the warmth of his body
under his jacket. Her hands didn't feel quite so cold any
more. In fact, she was really very comfortable; the broad
back in front of her was a solid windbreak and she
watched the strands of fly-away fair hair above her face.

He doesn't need a helmet to be seen, she thought; the
moon touches his hair with silver, like flickering fireflies.
She smiled at her imaginings and watched the road ahead
through half-closed eyes. It seemed an ethereal shadowy
world, lit with soft flashes of silver through a filmy mist.

The dreaminess ended slowly as she felt the motor
change and they turned into a narrow road. Distant
sounds were gradually more audible as they neared a
large house. Caroline sighed. Apparently the party was
in full swing. She almost wished they could go back to
the empty roads and keep riding into the quiet night.

She slowly dismounted after David and handed him
the helmet.

'All right?' he asked.

'Oh, yes.' She smiled up at him. 'That was lovely. I've
never ridden on a motorcycle before, and now I understand why people like it so much—especially at night.'

She could hear, rather than see, his answering smile.
'Good. I quite agree.' He turned away to direct Andrew
to a space beside the other cars.

Caroline looked up at the house. It was very large,
with lights on in every window. There didn't seem to be
any nearby neighbours; the noise would not be bothering
anyone else.

In spite of herself, she was interested to see Dr
Hunter's home. Following the sound of distant laughter,
she found a kitchen at the end of the central hallway. It
seemed very large, but it was difficult to see because of
the number of people leaning on the counters and chairs.
One couple was trying to dance on the top of the large
table.

As she turned to leave, she nearly collided with David
Hunter coming into the room carrying a tray of empty
glasses. 'Did you want something in particular?' His
friendly smile was oddly reassuring in the crush of
strangers.

'No, not really.' She wondered if he always had this
many people at his parties.

'If you would like some peace and quiet, my rooms
are upstairs. Turn right at the top, then left at the end
of the corridor. I'll bring something up.' With that brief
comment, he promptly disappeared in the general direction of the kitchen sink.

Shrugging lightly, Caroline looked for the stairs. She
wondered what 'something' he intended to provide;
whatever it was, she could always gracefully refuse.
Threading her way between chattering and laughing
people and away from the thudding pop music in the
sitting-room, she went up a wide staircase. It was
certainly quieter, although she could hear giggles and
muffled shrieks from behind some closed doors. There
seemed to be a lot of doors.

Turn right at the top, he had said. She passed several
doors and then looked left. It seemed there was a separate
wing to the house, not noticeable from the front. She
turned left and heard the unmistakable sounds of a
Habanera coming from a door on the left—not her
favourite music, but the stereo sounded powerful.

She stood, hesitating, outside a half-open door, looking around. There really wasn't anywhere else to go—
this was the end of the corridor. She pushed at the door
softly and stood watching the scene that met her eyes.

In the centre of the room, dancing energetically to the
blaring sound of *Carmen*, was the beautiful and completely naked body of the girl named Henry.

The fly-away auburn curls stopped moving abruptly and Caroline found herself being examined through squinting green eyes. The lovely body swayed a bit closer and the eyes peered closely at her.

'Hello. Who are you?'

CHAPTER THREE

'MY NAME is Caroline. And you are Henry?' Surprisingly, Caroline felt no embarrassment or discomfort. If this girl wanted to dance alone in the buff, that was her business. A swift thought passed through Caroline's mind. All that was missing was a rose in those pearly teeth.

'Yup. Henry, that's me. 'Orrible 'Enry!' A giggle punctuated by a hiccup accompanied this answer. 'Do you like mu-u-usic?'

'Yes, I do.' Caroline did wonder why this girl chose to dance in David Hunter's room, rather than downstairs. She doubted if anyone in the main rooms would have even noticed the lack of clothing.

'Lovely. . .luverly. . .whe-e-e-e. . .' Henry's pale body moved in a quick whirl around the room until she tripped on an overturned shoe and she fell, giggling, on to a narrow couch against one wall.

'That's enough, Henry.' The calm, deep voice behind her startled Caroline and she flushed, as David Hunter entered quietly and placed a tray he was carrying on the floor behind the door. She felt a sudden unease and backed away slightly. She watched him stride to the couch and firmly lift the girl upright in one swift movement.

As the pale arms circled his neck, accompanied by a deep-throated gurgle, Caroline felt an odd lurch in her stomach. Whatever was between these two people, she was certain she shouldn't be here. Before she could gather her thoughts and make an unobserved exit, she heard her name.

'Caroline, can you see any of her clothes around here?'

'Over there.' She pointed and his eyes followed her direction.

'Right then, Henry. Let's be off with you.' He added a pair of shoes to the collection and propelled the girl to the door.

Caroline stayed sitting on the floor, trying to make sense of what she had seen. Whose house was this? If it belonged to Dr Hunter, why did he live in 'rooms' apart from the rest of the house? If it belonged to Henry, why did he live here at all?

It was too much of a puzzle and Caroline gave up thinking about it. The music was still playing, although he had turned it down.

She stood up cautiously and looked over at the tray he had brought. Two bottles and some sandwiches. She looked more closely. Cheese. She was hungry so decided to try one and nibbled. Very good—granary bread. An inspection of the bottles offered a choice of white wine or apple juice. He had provided glasses so she poured out some of the apple juice and took her snack over to the stereo.

The music had stopped and she was examining the various knobs and switches when David Hunter returned.

'Did you find the food? Good.' He settled himself in the armchair and picked up a sandwich for himself. He pointed at the record collection. 'Pick out whatever you like.'

Noting that he had no intention of mentioning his lady-friend, Caroline scanned the labels. There was so much she would like to hear. From a lower shelf she picked out a disc of the Beethoven Sixth Symphony. They were out in the country, after all. He nodded and moved over to insert it in the machine. She watched him as he handled the equipment slowly so that she could follow his movements.

'I'll have to go back downstairs eventually but you can operate this on your own. The LP switch is here. OK?'

She nodded and moved back to the couch. Since he had taken the chair there was nowhere else for her to sit, so she curled up in the corner. Happily, he did not seem inclined to talk through the music. In fact he closed his eyes, stretched out his long legs and appeared to go to sleep.

She watched his face with interest. All the little lines around his eyes had relaxed and he looked much younger—younger even than she was herself. She could imagine how he would look, curled up in sleep. Don't be stupid, girl, she said to herself silently. Still, without those vibrant blue eyes he looked so much more vulnerable. Silly, that man would be vulnerable to nothing. He managed his world and everything in it by barely lifting a finger.

She deliberately turned her eyes away from the attractive face of David Hunter and slowly her mind drifted peacefully as the music filled the deepest corners of her mind.

As the music ended, David opened his eyes. 'Mmm. Good for the soul.' He poured himself some juice and pointed at the other bottle. 'The wine is for you, if you want it.'

She raised her still half-full glass. 'No, thanks. I thought it was for you.'

'I don't drink alcohol.' His statement was calm and matter-of-fact.

'Oh.' What was she supposed to say? Maybe he was a reformed alcoholic, and she didn't want to be rude. She certainly hoped her RMN training would give her the skills to respond properly to such forthright comments.

'No. My father was an alcoholic and that put me off it. Besides, I don't like the stuff.' Again his voice was completely expressionless.

There was nothing she could say. What *was* one supposed to say? She just looked at him solemnly.

He suddenly smiled at her, 'You'll get used to psych people. We always make outrageously frank statements about ourselves. You'll do the same yourself, you'll see.'

Caroline was doubtful. 'I don't know if I'll ever know enough about myself to be able to talk like that.' She added thoughtfully, 'I'd like to, though.'

'You will. It comes with the territory, as they say.' He

pulled himself upright in the chair. 'You can start now. For instance, you can tell me about your mad money.'

Caroline laughed. 'That's just a silly thing.' This was something she could talk about easily. 'When I first started going out with boys my aunt Betty always made me put some money, usually a pound note, in a secret pocket. She said it was my mad money. If I became angry at the boy, I would have enough money to get myself home on my own.' She laughed at the memory. 'I've always done it since then, out of habit really.'

'But the cost has gone up.' He grinned at her. 'Sounds very sensible to me. Your aunt Betty sounds a very wise woman.'

'Oh, yes, she is. . .was. . .' Caroline stumbled. This was much more difficult to talk about, but she had to learn some time. She looked over at the gently smiling man. After all, he is a psychiatrist, she thought. 'My aunt Betty is a wonderful person. She brought me up but now she's. . .she's ill.' Again she hesitated.

'Ill?' In his one word Caroline could hear concern and encouragement so she stumbled on.

'Yes. She became. . .ill. . .after I started nursing training.' She looked directly at his attentive face. 'I know it wasn't my fault. It's just one of those things that happens.' She smiled sadly. 'I would have done anything I could to help her. They said it was dementia and she eventually had to go into a nursing home last year. She's not very old—not even sixty yet.'

'I'm sorry. That can happen and I am very sorry indeed.' His concern sounded genuine and caring. Caroline felt her eyes sting and she brushed at them impatiently.

'I still find it hard to believe that she won't come back and be the person she always was. She was lovely, she really was.' She stopped talking and sniffed lightly.

'Where is she now?' His casual interest helped divert her thoughts from the past.

'In a home, in north London. It's near the hospital where I trained, but I'm a lot further away now. It's hard to get up there very often.'

He slowly unwound himself from the chair to stand

up. 'Well, we'll have to see if we can help a bit there. Do you know what ward you will be on?'

'Yes. Folkestone.' She looked up at him, wondering why this man should be interested in an old lady with dementia.

He gave her a broad smile. 'Excellent. I have a little bit of influence with the ward sister there. You see, that's one of my wards.'

'Oh.' For some reason, Caroline found this news unsettling, but the sensation was rather pleasant.

He nodded cheerfully. 'It's time I returned to my duties downstairs. Do you think you can handle that?' He pointed to the stereo. She nodded. 'Fine, I'll see you later, then.'

Caroline watched him leave, with a strangely let-down feeling. She had not mentioned Aunt Betty to anyone for years. It was a private sadness and she was surprised how relieved she felt just to mention her name to someone else. There was more she would like to tell this man—some of the funny memories, the sayings and incidents over the years. He would probably laugh at Aunt Betty's proverbs but, then again, he might not. She smiled to herself. So much for a personal introduction to the therapeutic effect of talking! She would just have to learn how to help give other people the same nice feeling, just by talking. And probably by listening, she thought, as she stifled a yawn.

Replacing her empty glass, she carefully switched the discs, choosing another Beethoven symphony. The man does have good musical taste, she thought as she curled up on the couch, using her folded coat as a pillow.

As he descended the staircase, David Hunter paused and looked at the few remaining occupants in the sitting-room. The room looked as if a small hurricane had swept through. He sighed. At least it was a good thing all the furnishings were rented. There was no sign of Henry. He assumed she had stayed in her room where he had left her. He could see Annabelle half asleep in a chair and Tracey was still trying to dance with a semi-conscious young man.

Making his way into the kitchen, he found Andrew at

the sink, methodically washing dishes. David noticed that an effort had been made to clear away some of the devastation.

'Thanks. I can clean up later.' David smiled at the young man.

Andrew nodded and dried his hands. 'It's time I took the girls home. Where's Caroline?'

'Upstairs. I'll tell her.' As he turned, David stopped. 'Can you find your way back to the hospital from here?'

'I think so. Straight to the roundabout, then left.'

'Yes, there's a sign there.' David walked quickly back upstairs, taking the treads two at a time.

He stood at the open door, watching the sleeping Caroline with an odd expression in his eyes—a mixture of puzzlement and tenderness. He moved forward quietly and touched her curled hand lightly.

'Caro.' His voice was barely above a whisper.

She did not stir at his touch or voice. He pulled a duvet from under the couch and gently laid it over her before silently retreating, closing the door behind him.

Andrew was waiting at the foot of the stairs and looked up at David, returning alone.

'She's asleep, Andrew. I didn't want to wake her.'

Andrew said nothing, merely watched David Hunter's face with a clear gaze.

David accepted his scrutiny and smiled softly. 'It's all right. I don't hurt sparrows.'

His words had been low and Andrew continued to look at him silently before nodding slowly. He turned and left, closing the door behind him carefully.

David listened to the departing vehicle for a few moments before rolling up his sleeves and heading in the direction of the kitchen.

'You're going soft, old man,' he muttered to himself. 'You saw this girl for the first time—when? Yesterday. Yes, not more than thirty-six hours ago. Now she's asleep upstairs in your sanctuary and that's precisely where you want her to stay. Yes, definitely soft!'

He started to hum a tune, recognised the Pastoral melody and laughed quietly. The clink and clatter of dishwashing continued to be accompanied by a quietly contented humming sound in the key of F major.

Caroline awoke slowly, to the delectable smell of fresh coffee and toast wafting through the house. She stretched her strangely tangled limbs and snuggled more deeply into a lovely warm duvet. Aunt Betty must have got up early. Was it Sunday? Of course it was Sunday; she could sleep in.

The aroma coming from the kitchen was too delicious to resist and she reluctantly opened one eye. She found she was looking at a scene of distant mountains reaching forever into a clear azure sky. Quite impossible, that sky. Her mind jerked suddenly. Mountains? She didn't have mountains at home. She opened both eyes and stared at the wall in front of her eyes. It was a skiing poster.

Slowly she remembered. This was the house where Dr David Hunter lived—a man who liked mountains. Mountains and music. She giggled softly. A strange combination—it sounded like a sugary film. She stopped giggling sharply. She was still in his house!

Caroline sat up abruptly. She was also still fully clothed. She didn't remember the duvet; he must have put it over her. Her cheeks flushed. She hadn't intended to fall asleep and she wondered where Andrew and the girls had gone.

She clambered out of the couch and rearranged her skirt and jumper. She felt all hot and sticky. Sleeping in one's clothes was uncomfortable; she couldn't remember having done it before. Her coat was neatly placed over a chair back and Caroline kicked herself mentally for not bringing even a comb. Well, she hadn't intended an overnight stay.

Opening the closed door, she looked out cautiously. The house was quiet except for a distant soft whistling as the occupant of the kitchen produced the lovely odours that had awakened her. Putting on her shoes, she tiptoed down the corridor, looking hopefully for a bathroom. Around the corner one door with a tiled floor was half open and she peeked in. Success!

There seemed to be an overabundance of towels and she looked at the closed shower curtain. She desperately needed a bath to get rid of the grubby feeling. Walking over to the curtain, she whisked it open and gasped with horror. There was a body in the bath!

Snorting at her own stupidity, she poked experimentally at the body. It was a full-clothed male, snoring softly and giving off an unmistakable odour of alcohol. It seemed the guests in this house slept wherever they fell. So much for the desired bath. A wash would have to do.

Closing the door and bolting it, hoping the prostrate occupant of the bath would remain asleep, she scrubbed as best she could. Finding what looked like a clean comb in the cabinet, she made an attempt to retie her hair but ended up with a loose plait. It would have to do.

Caroline wasted no time examining her shiny face, but threw her used towel into the hamper that seemed to be for laundry and made her way towards the tantalising smell of food. Again she was startled, as she looked around the corner of the kitchen door.

The room was clean and tidy, in marked contrast to her last view of it. David Hunter was seated at the large table, happily munching on a formidable-looking breakfast of juice, a mound of fruit, toast and that tempting coffee. He presented a multi-coloured picture of contentment—dressed in a jogging suit of an improbable shade of canary-yellow, with a turquoise jacket flung loosely over his shoulders. A mauve headband hung loosely under his chin. Caroline imagined the picture he must present on the road and giggled.

He looked up, waved a piece of toast and motioned to a chair. 'Good morning. Sleep well? Have some breakfast.'

'Good morning. Yes, I slept very well, thank you.' Caroline couldn't stop smiling. He looked so healthy and relaxed, grinning at her happily with a spot of honey on his chin. 'The coffee smell woke me up—it's lovely.'

'A personal blend. Try it.' He poured her a steaming mug, before popping some more bread in the toaster. 'How do you feel about early morning exercise?'

Caroline sipped at the coffee, to avoid answering immediately. She wasn't entirely sure what kind of exercise he had in mind. If it was running, she wasn't exactly dressed for it. 'The only exercise I would like is getting back home. I need a bath.' She blushed slightly. 'I don't usually sleep in my clothes.'

He waved his toast again. 'We have a perfectly good guest bathroom upstairs. Please feel free.' His grin widened. 'You can even sing, if you like.'

Caroline kept her eyes on the table and, taking a piece of toast, began to carefully spread on some of the honey. 'That might be a bit difficult. You see, there's a body in your bathtub.'

'A body?' It seemed a bit of toast had lodged in David Hunter's throat as he choked and stared at the demurely lowered glance across the table. He then caught the slightly quirking mouth in a face that looked up at him with bland innocence. 'Hmm. Well, Nurse Lawson, would you say that the body was still warm?'

'Oh, yes, Doctor, quite warm. Also fully clothed and probably pickled in alcohol.' She answered his grin with a wide smile.

'Well, in that case, there is nothing else for it. The inconvenient body must be removed.' He stood up and stretched his arms high above his head.

Caroline couldn't control a burst of laughter. His jogging trousers were a bright shade of pink!

'Now, now, mustn't laugh. This is protective colouring.' He started to swing his arms in wide arcs, carefully avoiding the laden table.

'But you look like. . .like a. . .like a peacock!' Caroline coughed slightly and she choked back her laughter. 'I'm sorry, but you do!'

He stopped his exercises and looked down at her with a strange look in his eye and said softly, 'I wonder how sparrows feel about peacocks.'

'I'm sorry?' Caroline wasn't sure if she had heard him properly and, if she had, she didn't understand what he meant. She looked up at him, brushing the tears of laughter from her eyes.

'Nothing.' He shrugged and smiled. 'How many

motorists do you think would miss this costume on the road?' He flexed his arms again. 'Meanwhile, to the matter at hand. Removal of said body from milady's bath.' With that, he loped quietly out of the door, with Caroline following behind, still munching toast. This she had to see. What was he going to do with that large, recumbent person?

She watched with interest as David pulled back the shower curtain and looked carefully at the sleeping man. He peered closely at the face and turned it slightly to one side.

'No, can't recall the face. This is definitely a new one.' He straightened up. 'Looks comatose, doesn't he?' He shook the lapels of the crushed jacket sharply, with no evident response from the wearer.

With a deep sigh, David steadied his feet, moving the bath mat to the side of the tub. 'Nothing for it, then. Just have to lift him out.'

Caroline watched with wide eyes as he slowly bent his knees and, reaching under the man's hips and arms, raised the heavy form to the edge of the bath, bent his knees again and suddenly shifted the weight to his own shoulders, straightened up and marched out of the room with the still unconscious man slung over his shoulders like a side of beef.

He turned outside the door, smiled broadly and bowed his head slightly while maintaining a firm hold on his burden. 'Your bath awaits, my lady.'

As she watched, he walked steadily down the corridor and disappeared through a door. A dull thud was heard as the unknown guest was unceremoniously dumped on protesting bedsprings.

Caroline let out a deep sigh. She didn't realise she had been holding in her breath. She really hadn't thought anyone could have lifted the man. Dr Hunter probably doesn't know his own strength, she thought to herself. You could be wrong again, Caroline, he probably does know his own strength but accepts it as calmly as he does everything else.

After a quick bath she did feel more refreshed and

made her way back to the kitchen. It was empty, with a place set for her with a dish of fruit, juice and a note. Wondering if he had gone off to do his running in multi-coloured splendour, Caroline first popped a slice of bread into the toaster before picking up the note.

'Am outside, preparing transport for return to hospital. Side door leads from kitchen to garage. D.'

Wondering what type of transport required preparations, she proceeded to eat breakfast—better here than snacks from the residence refrigerator. The food supplied in this house, whoever owned it, was far superior and she intended to make the most of the opportunity.

By the time she had licked the last bit of honey from her spoon, the pale winter sunlight was beginning to filter through the large kitchen window. She rinsed her dishes and looked out. There seemed to be a large unkempt garden outside, but it was difficult to see past the overgrown bushes bordering the high window.

Suddenly she heard the imperious ringing of a tinny bell. It had a vaguely familiar sound but she couldn't place it in her memory. Where had she heard that sound before?

She had it! It was a sound of childhood. With a delighted laugh, she reached for her coat and ran out of the side door, looking for the garage. She saw what resembled a giant gingerbread house. It was an elaborately gabled cottage, painted a warm shade of brown with sparkling white trim. All it needs, she thought, is for seven dumpy dwarfs to come marching out two by two. It was every child's dream playhouse and certainly didn't look like any garage she had ever seen.

A repeated ringing of the thin-sounding metallic bell took her around the corner of the fairy-tale cottage to find David Hunter standing over a very old and dilapidated bicycle.

'I don't believe it!' Her exclamation was a burst of childlike pleasure.

He looked up and grinned at her expression. 'I can't seem to get the handlebars to stay straight. Otherwise it should work all right.'

'It's beautiful.' She touched the pale green and white frame with delight.

He watched her glowing face with a twinkle in his eyes. 'Do you think you can stay upright on this?'

'Of course! I'll have you know I was the champion racer in my neighbourhood. That was a few years ago, though. . .' She stroked the cracking paint carefully. 'I fell off and broke my arm and wasn't allowed to ride any more.' She looked up at him. 'This one looks just like mine—it must be at least that old!'

'Could be. I found it in the old gardener's shed.' He gave the bell another quick twist. 'The bell is the most effective part of it. Good, isn't it?' He rang it again before allowing Caroline to take the machine away from him. 'Here, you'll break your neck!' He grabbed at her quickly, as she teetered on wobbling wheels.

'Get off! I can do it—watch!' With a defiant push away from him, she balanced precariously for a second before setting off at a considerable speed.

With a spurt, he set off beside her, pulling a colourful ski cap from his jacket pocket. 'Wait—you'll freeze. . .'

She stopped and turned back, laughing with pleasure. 'It's a lovely bike—just like mine.' She looked up at his face, flushed from his running. 'It wasn't this colour, though. It was a beautiful blue, just like y——' She stopped suddenly.

If he noticed her sudden silence, he said nothing, but waved the striped woollen hat at her. 'Put this on. It's colder outside than it seems.'

Caroline looked down at the offered hat, biting her lip. She had almost put her foot in it. Just the colour of his eyes, indeed. She was acting like a stupid child. She frowned at the ski cap. It had bright red stripes. She grimaced slightly and pulled the warm hat over her ears. She had to admit it did keep out the chill air.

She suddenly felt the need to get away from those warm blue eyes and deliberately set off rapidly, forcing him to run to keep up. That may not have been a clever move, she muttered to herself. He would think he'd been challenged to a race, and even on a bicycle she doubted if she could win against that large athletic frame.

It did not appear that David Hunter was interested in competition. He jogged along at a steady pace behind her until she had to slow for a small incline. He maintained his controlled rhythm and carried on past her, taking the hill with no visible effort.

'Some people are just too fit for their own good.' Caroline was again muttering to herself. She could feel her leg muscles beginning to complain about this unexpected exercise. 'Ah, this bit is better.'

She had come to the top of a slight rise and could see the yellow jersey of David Hunter beginning to set out on a level stretch of road. With a deep breath, she set off at speed. Surely she could catch him up.

The fable of the tortoise and the hare was holding true. Although she managed to shorten the distance between them by flying down the hill, the steady progress of the bright yellow runner continued along the flat road ahead. Giving up the chase, Caroline settled to a regular pedalling and looked around.

The morning sky was clear and the pale sun filtered through the clean branches of tall trees bordering the quiet brown fields. There was no sign of snow and a fresh wind was blowing gently in her face from the east. Slowly a feeling of exuberant well-being spread through her body and her fingertips and toes began to tingle with a pleasant warmth. It had been a long time since she had cycled, especially early in the morning, welcoming a winter day surrounded by the muted sounds of a slumbering countryside.

She started to sing lightly. She felt as if she were following a colourful bouncing ball in the distance as she kept the yellow-clad jogger in her sights. He looked a bit like a toy clown in the distance, with his pink trousers and yellow top.

'Follo-o-w the yellow bright man,' she carolled loudly, 'Fo-ollow the yello-o-ow bright man.' Her feet kept the regular beat. 'Fo-ollow, fo-ll-ow, fo-ll-ow, fo-ll-ow, fo-ll-ow the yellow bright man.'

She stopped for breath and started up again. 'I'm off to follow the man. That wonderful. . .' No, that didn't sound right. She couldn't think of a proper rhyme and continued in ringing tones. 'I know he's a wonder *because*. . .' this note was savoured to the full and she stopped cycling '. . .*because* of the wonderful things he does. Da da de de de de *dum*!'

Faint echoes of her clear singing echoed on the breeze and she laughed out loud. Pausing again to catch her breath, she could hear very faint sounds in the distance, underneath the cries of the high flying birds circling lazily overhead. She stopped and concentrated very hard. Very faintly the wind carried a melody across the fields to the edge of her hearing. Just as she thought her ears were playing tricks, she heard the delicate clear crystal notes.

Caroline smiled with pure pleasure and looked ahead to see if she had lost the yellow bounding man. No, David Hunter was leaning against a stile at the top of another steep hill. Caroline started to push the bicycle. She could get uphill faster walking and she must tell him, so he could listen to the beautiful sounds.

David watched her as she pushed the bicycle quickly, smiling broadly up at him. As if she has a delicious secret, he thought, and wondered what private delight might light up the face of this black-haired girl, dressed in the colours of the sleeping fields with an absurd red bobble bouncing on her striped cap. He could feel the fresh wind on his face and slowly stretched his long legs as he balanced on the wooden fence post.

He couldn't remember when he had felt so alive and wondered if this feeling just might have something to do with a brown-eyed girl who liked to sing in the bath and on bicycles, could dream to Beethoven and hear words in drumbeats, and who had an inner stillness that had reawakened a forgotten power within himself.

He looked down at the uplifted face flushed with excitement, as Caroline burst out, 'Can you hear them, David? Can you?' The use of his name had slipped out unconsciously.

'What do you hear, Caro?' His voice held a note of tenderness.

She had heard the diminutive form of her name but

was too eager to share her experience to think about it. 'The bells! Listen. . .there are bells ringing!'

He listened carefully. She was right. Very faintly, on the edge of the wind, he could hear the village church bells. He smiled down at her. It was Sunday, but he couldn't remember having heard them before. He started to speak but she put a finger against her lips briefly.

Caroline was filled with a sense of wondrous enchantment. The resonant peals of the deep-toned bells carried on the morning air echoed the regular rhythm of her own breathing. As she looked up at the weather-browned face above her and saw his understanding, she felt a shiver of pure joy. She knew that this was a magical moment and perhaps never again would she feel as deeply happy as she did in this very instant. She looked up with her heart shining in her eyes.

A fleeting caress on her trembling mouth seemed a natural part of her bewitchment. Without thinking, she answered the light pressure by moulding her lips to his, tasting a soft sweetness that made her long to cling to him tightly. She knew that if she didn't hold on to him she would be carried off with the sounds on the wind. Only his arms could keep her from flying high above the fields to disappear up among the clouds, leaving the safety of the earth forever. Safety. . .

Suddenly her eyes widened and David saw the fear fluttering in their depths as she quickly withdrew from him. Damn, he thought. He should have remembered how touch frightened this sparrow. He hadn't intended to kiss her—it had just seemed right to share her moment of happiness.

As Caroline backed away, he smiled broadly and spoke in a light, cheerful tone. 'That's what hearing church bells does to a man—we come over all romantic.'

'Oh.' She was flustered. She had forgotten where she was and who she was with, and struggled to still the sudden trembling in her knees as well as the familiar fluttering feeling that clutched at her chest. She could hear his voice speaking in a normal conversational tone and she took a few deep breaths.

'Those are the bells from the local church. Our poor

vicar has three parishes and has to commute between them. I think our service is at eight-thirty before he has to whip off to the next one.'

Caroline had regained a firm hold on herself, as well as the bicycle. 'Do they have a choir?'

'I don't know. Why?' What was this girl on about now?

'I thought perhaps you might sing in it.' She knew she was chattering to stop herself dashing away from this man who caused her to feel so unsettled.

'Me?' The full-hearted sound of his laughter was carried away in the wind. 'My choir singing ended when I was twelve and my voice broke.' He grinned at her. 'Other than the occasional bar-room knees-up, that is.'

Caroline managed a tentative smile in response and he breathed a silent sigh of relief. He had half expected her to take off at top speed. At least she hadn't run away from him, but it was now time to let the frightened little brown bird flutter her wings.

He started to jog on the spot. 'Ready for more cross-country cycling?'

Caroline nodded. She found his abundant energy a bit overwhelming, but when he stopped moving dangerous things could happen. She started pedalling down the opposite side of the hill and waited for him to surge ahead at the bottom.

It seemed he had changed his running programme and kept a steady pace beside her bicycle on the now level road. At the roundabout he pointed their direction and they kept an equal pace until the gates of Castleview came in sight.

Caroline slowed down. She felt she ought to say something to this man but there were no words. 'Thank you for a lovely ride' sounded strange and hardly covered the range of her confused feelings.

Well aware of her uncertainty, David marched up to the door of the residence, stood to attention and gave her a brief salute. 'End of the escorted service. Door-to-door personal delivery, ma'am.'

'Thank you.' Caroline smiled and climbed off the bicycle. She gave the silver bell a quick ring. 'It does

work well. It was nice to. . .ride a bicycle again.' She
hesitated, not knowing what else she should say.

'Any time.' He grinned and held out his hand, palm
outstretched. She looked confused and he pointed to her
head.

With a self-conscious laugh, she took off the bright ski
cap and felt the cold wind whip through her hair. She
moved to the opened door and turned back to see him
mount the bicycle and couldn't resist a loud giggle. His
addition of the red-striped hat to the yellow jersey and
pink trousers somehow looked quite appropriate as he
rode away on the green and white bicycle. He gave her a
brief wave and left in a swift swirl of kaleidoscopic
colour.

Caroline went into the silent residence and regained
the precious privacy of her room. How could so much
have changed since she was last in her own room? It
seemed the whole world had changed into a rainbow.
Did she look any different? She looked in the mirror.
Had it really been only twelve hours since she had looked
at her own reflection adorned with the red scarf and the
earrings? She quickly checked her pocket. They were
still safely there.

Placing the red silk square on the bureau, she looked
at it with a frown. That was the sort of thing that
happened when she wore red. She ended up sleeping in
strange men's houses and getting kissed to the sound of
church bells. Her cheeks flamed at the memory of that
magical moment and she touched the edges of her lips
with trembling fingertips. Magic or sorcery, she thought,
the charming David Hunter would not be casting any
more spells over her. He was just a handsome man who
manhandled naked women, sang like an angel and kissed
strange girls on bicycles.

It was time to turn off the enchantment and get back
to the real world. Indeed, it was most definitely time to
get to work on the long list of diagnostic terminology
before Monday morning.

CHAPTER FOUR

As SHE walked briskly over to Folkestone Ward in the morning, Caroline was aware of feeling nervous, but felt relieved at actually beginning the work she had come to do. As she opened the swing door leading to the unit, an atmosphere of bustling activity surrounded her and she began to relax. There were the same sounds as in any hospital ward, with the faint clatter of breakfast being dished out in a kitchen, the soft voices of nurses looking for supplies or answering telephones, and the clink of a medicine trolley being wheeled on linoleum floors.

Caroline sniffed the air; she could detect the fresh smell of hospital disinfectant and smiled to herself. Some aspects of nursing jobs never changed; not everything would be unfamiliar.

During the morning shift report she sat silently, listening to the brief outline of each patient the night sister was giving. She knew this was largely for her benefit as the new staff member and she concentrated on trying to remember the important points. There were so many names and the diagnostic labels came so quickly. Caroline resolved to get at the classification list again after work; it was going to be needed.

After report she followed the energetic staff nurse around. Ruby was cheerful and practical and talked quietly to Caroline as they did a round of the ward together.

'We have about thirty at the moment—a full house. We're rarely less than that and for any extras we have to put up beds in the side alcoves.' She was bustling into the linen cupboard and piled stacked clean sheets into Caroline's waiting arms.

'We don't make most of the beds—the men can do it for themselves. But there are some who need a bit of help. Like Mr Lawrence here. . . Good morning, how did you sleep last night?' They had entered a four-bed dormitory where an elderly man was perched on the end of a narrow bed, still in his crumpled pyjamas. The other occupants of the room had disappeared to have breakfast in the dining-room.

Caroline remembered that the night report had said that Mr Lawrence had slept well, but the patient was not supporting that view.

'Terrible, Miss Ruby, terrible. It was the voices again. . .they wouldn't leave me alone. All night they were at me. . .' His watery pale blue eyes looked wanly up at the bustling staff nurse.

'I'm sorry to hear that, Mr Lawrence. What do you think we can do to help you get a proper sleep?' She was quietly and efficiently stripping the bed around the old gentleman, then stood him up briefly and slung the bedding into the waiting wheeled laundry hamper. Caroline could see the sheets were completely soaked. So incontinence was going to be a nursing problem; this was familiar.

'I'll help Mr Lawrence with his bath, if you can redo the bed, please, Caroline.' Ruby was leading the patient slowly out of the room.

Caroline moved to start making the bed, after smoothing out the waterproof mattress cover, and looked around for the antiseptic cleaning supplies. She found them in a utility-room at the end of the corridor and went about the work of housekeeping. It was good to have her hands busy but she felt awkward out of uniform. She told herself she could make her own bed without being in a nursing uniform—making someone else's shouldn't be so very different.

After distributing piles of clean linen to the other patients' beds in the dormitory, she helped Ruby walk the washed and dressed Mr Lawrence to the dining-room and found him a corner seat. She went up to the counter to get him a tray after asking and finding out that he wanted 'the lot, dear, the lot'. Keeping in mind his probably shaky dentition, she filled a plate with scrambled eggs, sausage and tomato. He grinned his appreciation of her choice and happily settled to enjoy his meal.

Caroline looked around, uncertain as to what was expected of her now. She couldn't sit down; she certainly couldn't eat breakfast here. What was she to do? There hadn't been any patient assignment or duty roster given. She felt a small moment of anxiety. She had no direction. No one had told her what to do.

She gave herself a firm shake. Don't be daft, woman. You're a nurse. You can think for yourself. Ruby had disappeared after leading Mr Lawrence to the table. Caroline looked around. The room was fairly large and was filled with at least twenty-five men, all eating breakfast at small tables. She looked more carefully. Some of the patients were not eating, simply staring down at their plates. She looked around to see if there were other staff members around. It was impossible to tell if any of the men were staff; no one wore uniforms. Any woman *must* be staff. She saw a middle-aged woman sitting at a far table, buttering toast.

Well, thought Caroline, if she can help patients with their breakfast, so can I. She looked around for someone not eating and noticed a middle-aged man, still in his pyjamas and dressing-gown, seated beside a far table by the window, looking out with his breakfast tray untouched. She thought he looked vaguely familiar, but then he probably just looked more 'normal' than some of the others. His hair was carefully combed and his dressing-gown neatly tied. His face looked very sad and lost.

Well, she said silently to herself, you might as well get on with it—this is why you have come here. Caroline approached the gentleman slowly and stood beside his chair to look out of the window. The scene was bleak. The day was grey and the view of a small patch of garden looked desolate in its emptiness.

She stood quietly for a few moments before speaking. 'Winter can be a sad time, can't it?'

She continued to look out of the window. If he wished to speak, that was fine. If he wished to remain silent, that she was also prepared to accept. Gradually she felt more relaxed; she liked to look out of windows, and perhaps he just liked to be on the edge of a group as she did. She felt his eyes on her face but she did not turn, merely allowed him to look at her.

He must have reached a judgement because he finally spoke. 'Not always.' His voice was rough and low, but the softness with which he spoke lent a sadness to his words. The harshness could have been because of disuse or contained emotion, Caroline could not tell. She turned to look at him.

His face was deeply lined, but the strong bone-structure still showed through the greyish skin. His eyes were ringed with shadows, but Caroline again had the feeling that she had seen his face before. She smiled tentatively at him.

'May I sit down?' She motioned with her hand to an empty chair at the corner of his table.

'My pleasure.' The formality of his words reinforced her impression that this man was perhaps a bit 'different' from the others. She felt a growing curiosity, but held it in check. He seemed a very private man and she felt she must move carefully. It had become important not to hurt this man who seemed so sad.

'Did you not like your breakfast?' Caroline couldn't think of anything else to say. She groaned silently at herself. What an inane thing to say. If he had liked it, he would have eaten it, wouldn't he? Almost as bad as talking about the weather, and she'd already done that! She was rapidly running out of conversational small talk.

As if he sensed her thoughts, the man smiled very briefly at her and tapped the edge of an empty teacup with the tip of a long finger. Caroline's gaze caught on his hands. They were the most beautiful hands she had ever seen and looked much younger than the man's face. The fingers were slim but strong, and his wrists, un-covered by his sleeves, were also muscular but slender.

Caroline reached for a teapot to fill his cup, but his long finger moved quickly. 'After you, my dear.' His rough voice was barely audible but quite firm.

'Oh.' Caroline was uncertain. She wasn't sure she was supposed to be drinking tea with the patients, and she didn't want to break any rules, certainly not on her first day on the ward. But she couldn't refuse his offer. He seemed such a gentleman and she couldn't insult him.

She poured herself a cup and filled another one for him. She noted that he added milk later—just as Aunt Betty always had, Caroline thought. This memory was surprisingly comforting and she smiled at the gentleman opposite her and contentedly stirred her tea.

If psychiatric nursing included drinking cups of tea with distinguished-looking old gentlemen, then Caroline was going to like it. Unusual, but very pleasant indeed. She smiled at him, said 'Thank you' and they sat in companionable silence looking out at the courtyard.

Two observers were watching this scene with amusement and surprise. The amused glance belonged to David Hunter, the surprise to the ward sister standing beside him, at the entrance to the dining area.

'Hmm. It seems we have a winner here, Meg,' David Hunter's voice was low. 'Do you see what I see?'

'I do indeed. And if I didn't see it myself, I wouldn't credit it. The old gentleman has refused all food and drink in the company of others.' Margaret Clarke's voice was filled with delight. 'It's about time he unwound a bit.'

'You mustn't underestimate the power of a pair of delightful brown eyes, Margaret. They can be a powerful medicine.' His glance rested on the shining black head angled slightly towards the patient as the two watched a bird pick at a sloping tree branch outside the window.

'Brown are they, then? And trust you to know that!' The teasing tone sounded friendly; the ward sister and senior registrar had worked together for three years and understood each other very well.

'It's my job to know such things, my dear Meg. And I know that pair is exceptionally fine.' A note in his voice caused a swift upward glance from his colleague and the hint of a raised brow, but no comment. She smiled to herself, looked once more over at the new student and moved off towards the office, leaving Dr Hunter standing in the doorway.

He looked slowly around, noticing where everyone was seated, who was not eating and how each patient was dressed, without a conscious awareness of his detailed observations. Such swift mental note-taking was now a habit, performed without deliberate thought, but there was nothing careless in his returning glance to Caroline. He wondered how she had picked out that particular patient. He smiled as the glimmer of an idea began to grow at the back of his mind.

The smile widened and David Hunter chuckled quietly. A muttered 'It just might work' was overheard.

'Talking to yourself then, Doctor? That's the first sign, they say.'

'What?' David turned and grinned at the wide grin under the tousled head of Terry. 'Oh, hello, lad—got back all right, then? Yes. I've been thinking.'

'Dangerous stuff, thinking. Better watch yourself!'

'True.' He laughed easily. 'Do you think you could borrow the drums, or part of them, from the Neighbour?'

'Might do. What have you got in mind?' The face under the mop of fair hair looked up with a questioning glance.

David's smile took on a mischievous air. 'It has occurred to me that a little bit of music therapy might be useful for us on Folkestone. What do you think, Terry?'

The boy's expression became thoughtful. 'You already know what I think about that. Those drums keep me sane.' He paused and looked around at the patients drifting out from their breakfast. 'Were you thinking of anyone else in particular?'

David watched the elderly gentleman now quietly walking back in the direction of his dormitory, leaving Caroline seated at the table. He received a courteous nod in response to his cheerful greeting. 'Good morning, Mr Vanijek.'

Terry was silent as the patient passed out of earshot. 'Him? The word has it that he's the real thing. If you plan to get him going, I'll have to sharpen up—he'll be way out of my league.' He left David Hunter with an energetic wave, 'I'll let you know what I can get.'

David nodded and continued on his way to the office. He wasn't sure exactly what he intended, but Anton

Vanijek was a treatment problem. It just might take an unorthodox approach to reach that particular patient. At least it was worth a try, he thought, and put his still unformed plans aside. There were another sixty patients under his care and he hurried to a meeting with the ward sister to hear the weekend report.

After her tea-drinking companion had left, with a slight bow to her, Caroline felt much more relaxed in her new working environment. At least the patients had seen her and perhaps recognised the strange face as a new staff member.

As she followed the drift of the patients out of the dining-room, she decided to take a tour of the ward to refresh her memory. All of the new students had visited the wards earlier and she remembered the L-shaped building had housed two four-bed dormitories at either end, with smaller rooms on each side of a central corridor. She didn't remember seeing what was in the 'foot' of the L, at the western end of the building.

She walked down to the end, pausing at each door as she passed. At one room she noticed a patient having difficulty with his bed-making and she moved in to help him, after quietly introducing herself. They completed the task in silence and she moved on to the next dormitory. Occasionally she received a nod in response to her greeting. Others ignored her, which she accepted as an understandable reaction. She was the new person here and would need to earn their trust.

At the end of the central corridor she found a closed double door with glass panel inserts. The glass was dusty but she could see through to the space beyond. It seemed to be a long, wide room with little furniture. She could see two broken beds in a far corner and a stack of plastic chairs, but little else.

'Not much in there.' A young, friendly voice caused her to turn quickly.

'Oh, hello!' Caroline was surprised to see the cheerfully smiling face of the boy who had been playing the drums in the restaurant.

'Hello. Welcome to the nut-house.' He noted her

surprise with a wide grin. 'This used to be a workshop, so they tell me. No use now—just storage.'

Caroline swallowed her astonishment at seeing the boy here. She guessed he must be a patient and she immediately assumed the friendly professionalism that had become second nature to her. In similar situations in medical nursing she had found honesty was the best policy and hoped the same rule would apply here.

She smiled at him, 'Are you staying here on Folkestone?' Honesty might be best but she couldn't be certain how forthright such truthfulness could be. She wasn't quite ready to use the term 'patient' directly.

'Yeah, one of the regulars, that's me.' He seemed unabashed. 'My name's Terry.'

'I know. Dr Hunter told me your name. My name is Caroline.' She felt it was only courteous to offer her name, as he had seen her in the restaurant. 'I enjoyed your playing very much. I thought the whole group was good.' Her compliments were genuinely felt and Terry's face lit up with pleasure.

'Thanks. Life is easier with the drums—they don't talk back.' His eyes lowered briefly and Caroline said nothing. She sensed an underlying tension in the boy and realised that she had transferred him in her mind from 'normal' to 'psychiatric patient'. Now she was looking for signs of illness with her eyes and ears alert for signs of abnormality. She only wished she knew what these might be. Terry looked perfectly normal to her.

'You seemed to talk very well with your drums.' She remembered his playing and her own reaction. Somehow she wanted to encourage Terry to continue talking to her, but how should she do that without 'talking back'? She wondered what he had meant by his comment.

Terry glanced up at her face, gave her an intent look and merely nodded.

In an effort to keep the conversation going, Caroline tried another approach. 'Can you tell me what happens now—after breakfast? This is my first day here.' Perhaps if he felt he could be of help to her, the boy would feel less pressured to talk.

'Sure. Now we go to the ward group.' He seemed

willing to act as her guide and continued to chatter easily
as they returned to the central area. 'Everyone is supposed to go to the day-room to discuss whatever's been
going on since last Thursday. We do this Mondays and
Thursdays. It's always the same thing—you'll see.'

Pleased that he had accepted her suggestion, Caroline
willingly followed him to the large room next to the
dining area. It was beginning to fill with patients and
staff.

Terry obviously shared her preference for back-row
seats and she accompanied him to two chairs placed
slightly behind a high-backed arm chair. She noticed
that all of the seats on the edge or back of the group
were filled first. She smiled inwardly. It would appear
that psychiatric patients did not wish to be the centre of
attention.

She immediately had to revise this opinion as a
prominent front seat was taken by a thin young man who
moved very quickly and sat twisting his fingers con-
stantly in an unceasing pattern on the buttons of his
cardigan.

So absorbed was she in watching the jerking movements of this patient that Caroline was startled to see
David Hunter purposefully striding in her direction. She
looked up sharply and felt her cheeks flush slightly as
she met his clear blue eyes and acknowledged his slight
nod in her direction. He then nodded and smiled at
Terry seated beside her, and casually lowered himself
into the deep armchair in front of them.

Mentally kicking herself for her reaction to his arrival,
Caroline settled herself to listen, watch and learn. Of
course he would be here, and the large chair in front of
her seemed to be the only one still empty. She noted she
was again slightly behind his very broad shoulder. This
was becoming a familiar and quite comfortable position.
She wondered if Terry also looked for this type of
protection, as he had chosen the seat directly behind the
armchair, probably knowing David Hunter sat there.

Keeping her eyes on the circle of patients and staff,
Caroline was acutely aware of the fine, fair hair inches
from her face. She folded her hands quietly in her lap,

resisting a rather odd impulse to tidy a fly-away lock that had fallen over the strong cheek-line she could just see out of the corner of her eye.

She became absorbed in the conversation going on in the group. The restless patient in the front row seat was named Bob and seemed to be complaining about the hospital food. Caroline smiled; his opinions seemed perfectly normal to her. All hospital patients complained about the food. She noticed the ward sister seated with a small notepad on her lap. She appeared to be taking brief notes, as Bob spoke.

'The food's always terrible.' This support for Bob came from an overweight middle-aged man with a florid complexion. 'What I want to know is—what do you intend to do about the thief around here?'

'What do you mean, Fred?' asked a young man whom Caroline had seen helping to dress one of the patients and had assumed was a staff member. The question was spoken mildly.

'I mean—whoever's been nicking stuff has got to be stopped. That's what I mean!' Fred's face had become even redder.

'Have you lost something?' The young staff member remained calm.

'I had a good wristwatch nicked last night—and I want it back! Cost me a packet and I didn't come here to get robbed in my sleep!' The angry voice was loud and harsh.

Looking around the group, Caroline noted the general lack of interest in the large man's complaint. Some patients were looking at their feet or out of the window; others were watching with mild curiosity, and two or three others, including Mr Lawrence in a corner, seemed to be fast asleep. Any staff members she could identify seemed equally unconcerned about Fred's comments. David Hunter had remained relaxed and immobile with his large, strong hands laid casually on the arms of his chair.

Perhaps minor theft was a not unusual problem here, Caroline thought. She had seen no locked doors, other than the drug cupboard. The ward office had a latch that she supposed could be locked, if necessary. Otherwise, the main door and all the patient rooms seemed to be always open.

'Has anyone else lost anything?' Another staff member directed the question to the group as a whole. This was the middle-aged woman Caroline had seen in the dining-room.

'Yes, yesterday my razor disappeared.' The speaker was a short man dressed neatly in a shirt and tie, under a clean woollen cardigan. After he spoke, Caroline could see that he looked unshaven, but then so did a number of other patients.

Checking quickly around the edges of the group she caught a glimpse of her tea-drinking companion. He looked clean-shaven and had dressed in a clean blue shirt. She suddenly had an odd wish that he were not wearing bedroom slippers. Somehow people looked more defenceless and like sick patients without proper shoes. Catching his glance, she smiled slightly but received no visible response. She realised that already she was wishing this man to be well.

Returning her attention to the group, Caroline kept the unsmiling face on the edge of her vision. He appeared quite uninterested in the preoccupation of the group with the topic of disappearing items from the ward.

'What about the kettle, then?' This question came from another patient and was directed towards the ward sister who nodded in response but said nothing.

'Has anyone seen the electric kettle? It was here last Wednesday.' The male nurse who had answered Fred's original question directed his comment to all the group members.

There were a few murmured 'No's and some shuffling of feet, but most members remained silent. Gradually the silence spread and enveloped the whole group. Caroline could feel her legs tingle and she longed to twitch her feet. Why was everyone so silent? Why didn't someone say something?

As the silence lengthened, she looked over at the ward sister who sat calmly watching the patients. Surely she would say something to keep the conversation going.

Even Dr Hunter remained still and silent. How could he be so relaxed, when her own fingers were clasped tightly in her lap to keep herself from shuffling and moving in the quiet? Even Terry seated beside her seemed unconcerned.

'I've had enough of this!' Bob exclaimed loudly as he rose abruptly from his chair. 'I've got work to do and this is just a waste of time!' He walked with jerky steps out of the circle and his footsteps could be heard heading for the unit door.

Caroline breathed quietly; she was relieved to have the silence broken. It had made her anxious and she realised that most groups of people normally kept talk continuous. Maybe silence made other people nervous as well— it had certainly bothered Bob. As the staff members remained mute, other patients began to leave the room.

It seemed as if Bob's departure had ended the meeting and others now felt free to leave. Caroline wondered if this was considered to be group therapy. She didn't see how it could be, if most people had said nothing.

As she watched the circle of chairs slowly empty she wondered what 'work' Bob was doing. Turning sideways to let Terry leave, she smiled up at him.

'Why don't you come over to OT?' His suggestion was friendly. 'That's where most of us spend the morning. It's not so bad.'

'I'd like to.' She was grateful for any suggestion that could provide her with some structure. It was difficult to do the expected thing without some direction from others. 'I'll ask Sister.'

David Hunter was still seated, casually relaxed, in front of her. Caroline smiled tentatively at him as she slid off her chair. His cheerful nod was reassuring. Perhaps it was all right for her to leave, although the other staff members had remained seated.

She moved over to where the ward sister was still sitting; she had closed her notebook and seemed to be waiting for all of the patients to leave.

'Excuse me, Sister.' Caroline's respectful approach was the result of her years of training. All staff were treated with courtesy and in this setting Caroline felt

acutely aware of her own position as a beginning learner.
'May I go to occupational therapy with Terry? I'd like to
see the programme.'

'Of course, Caroline,' Margaret Clarke answered
briskly. 'That's an excellent idea. Your first day on the
ward is intended as orientation and you will recognise
several of our people there.'

The older nurse watched her most recent student
eagerly follow the young patient out of the room. Within
an hour of being on the ward this young nurse had begun
to establish relationships with two patients and was
functioning well with a minimum of imposed direction.
David Hunter's comment seemed to be justified; this
young woman showed all the signs of being a rapid
learner.

The building that housed the occupational and physio-
therapy departments was a fair distance from Folkestone.
Going through the workshop doors, she made a mental
note to wear a heavier cardigan the next day, even if it
upset her plans to look 'professional'.

The warmth of the large room was welcome and she
stopped to look around at the wide array of tables, piled
cartons against the walls and the cluster of machinery at
the end of the room. The whole area was brightly lit and
there were some room dividers used to provide individual
working places along one side of the room. These were
low enough for an observer to see each working surface
clearly.

Terry was beckoning to her from the far end and she
walked quickly towards him.

'This is Eric, the OT supervisor. Eric, this is
Caroline—she started today on Folkestone.' Following
Terry's rapid-fire introduction, Caroline found her hand
being shaken firmly by a large man with deep bushy
eyebrows and a bristling moustache.

'Welcome, Nurse. Anything you would like to know,
please ask.' The slightly guttural voice suited the broad-
boned face and slightly Slavic cheekbones. He wore a
leather apron and had rolled up his shirt-sleeves. The

hint of a European accent reinforced Caroline's impression of a man whom Aunt Betty would call 'a man of the earth, a hewer of wood'. Caroline warmed to the kindly glint under those heavy brows.

'Thank you, I will.' She smiled broadly at him before turning to where Terry was eagerly unpacking a small box of tools.

'This is what I'm making—it's just a first effort. Eric's going to teach me the lathe, I hope.' He was holding a long piece of wood with a slightly tapered end. 'So far, I'm just shaping with the shaver, but I want to be able to turn edges.'

'This looks like it might be a stick for drums. Is it?' She couldn't be certain what he was trying to make.

'Almost right. Here.' He pulled out a deep drawer to show her several blocks of wood. 'I want to make these into hollow gourds. Each will have a different sound.' He grinned at her expression. 'Like bottles filled with water—you know, different amounts of water make a different note when you blow over the top?' Caroline nodded. 'So, hollow wooden gourds of different sizes and shapes will make different sounds when struck—a new musical instrument!'

Caroline smiled at his enthusiasm. Terry was indeed a clever young man, as David Hunter had said. 'You'll have a lot of work to do. How many do you want to make?'

'I don't know yet. It depends what they sound like. My first efforts will probably be disasters.' He seemed undeterred by the prospect of failure and Caroline again wondered why he was a patient here.

Her unspoken question was partly answered as the boy rolled up his sleeves to begin work. His lower arms were covered with dozens of thin scars, some fading, others more recent, and some still in the early stages of healing.

Caroline had seen razor-cut scars before but never so many together. So it seemed Terry had made several suicidal gestures and had done so over a long period of time, judging by the number of healed cuts. Some also looked as if they had needed stitches to close. She felt a deep compassion for this likeable boy. He must be very unhappy to have inflicted such pain on himself.

She said nothing and, as Terry had his head turned, searching for a wood shaver, he was not aware of her observation.

'I'll let you get on with your work, Terry.' Caroline was glad to hear her voice remained calm and friendly. She needed time to absorb this new information about him. 'I'd like to take a look around, if that's all right.'

'Sure, OK. See you later.' He had found the shaver and was carefully beginning to move it over his length of wood.

Caroline turned and surveyed the room. Most of the workplaces now were occupied and she could see several of the Folkestone patients. She noticed the restless Bob energetically pounding nails into a long wooden plank. Almost unconsciously, she looked for her breakfast companion and found him, at the edge of a long worktable.

He seemed to be sorting out piles of something, so she slowly moved along the wall to get a closer look. She did not want to appear overly curious so she stopped to look at the work of several patients and smiled or made some comment as she passed.

As she neared the distinguished-looking gentleman she felt her heart sink slightly. He was slowly and methodically sorting coloured cards—they looked like children's Easter cards—into piles and carefully placing one of each into small cardboard containers. He then placed the filled boxes on one side and started another. It seemed such a sad sight to Caroline—his strong slender hands employed in such mind-numbing activity.

She sighed lightly and moved away, behind the patients' line of sight, and looked out through the scratched glass of a metal-framed window. Her eyes were not focused on the grey day outside as she thought of the inconsistencies in what she was seeing and feeling.

She frowned to herself and looked up to see the supervisor watching her, with a slight smile on his face. He moved across an aisle between the tables towards her, looking at the patients' work as he passed. He spoke to some and nodded to anyone who lifted a head to look at him. Most patients seemed to be concentrating solely on the task before them as if the work needed all of their attention.

'Hello, Nurse.' The tall, heavy man looked down at Caroline. 'Come, I wish to show you. . .you will like, I think.' He pointed towards the end of the room and Caroline followed him, curious to see what he wanted of her. She was aware he had observed her frown and she did not want him to think she disapproved of his therapy unit. They passed through a door into an office area cluttered with papers, boxes and bits of machinery.

'Here, you sit, please.' He began to rummage behind the desk as Caroline perched herself gingerly on the edge of a chair across from a menacing-looking power drill lying on top of a pile of cartons.

As he shifted boxes, the supervisor kept talking in a serious tone. 'I see you watch and you are. . .puzzled. . .maybe?'

'A bit.' Caroline felt this was an understatement, but she had to agree that she certainly felt confused. She added, 'It just seemed that the. . .work. . .' she hesitated over the word '. . .seems so. . .basic. . .for some of the patients. I mean, it must be very good for them, I suppose, but——' She stopped. She could hear herself beginning to sound as if she was objecting to this man's therapy programme.

'I understand.' He was lifting a large box with ease and looked over at her. 'For some, it is all they can do— to perform a simple task. For others, it is all they choose to do—to fill in the empty time.'

He took a small key out of his trouser pocket and lifted a long narrow box from a bottom shelf. 'Now I show you. This is *my* occupational therapy!' He chuckled lightly as he placed the box on Caroline's lap.

It was not heavy and, as he unlocked the small padlock, Caroline had a feeling that she was about to see something very important. She watched with interest as he lifted the lid and carefully unwrapped the clean towels lining the box.

'Oh!' She gazed at the perfection of an exquisitely

crafted violin. There were no strings and the surface had
not yet been finished, but the carving and the woodwork
were very fine. She touched the elegant curve of a side
wall with a soft stroke of her fingers. 'This is beautiful,
Eric, truly beautiful.'

He beamed his pleasure. 'The wood is good. It came
from the storm, you remember?' She nodded. The
destruction of many trees in this area of the country had
been widespread.

'We do not often get such good material here. I saved
it—waited for it to dry and season right.' He sat down
and picked up the instrument in his massive hands. 'This
is for him.'

'Him?' asked Caroline.

'Yes. I saw you watching him, when you were frowning.' Eric was still looking down at the violin and was
rubbing at the edges of the carving carefully.

Caroline flushed slightly. Eric was still talking, partly
to himself. 'He may never play it. That will be for him
to decide. Still, I give it, when it is finished.'

'Give it?' Did he mean the distinguished-looking
gentleman? Then, just as Eric spoke again. Caroline's
memory finally fell into place.

'Yes, to Maestro Vanijek. It is for him. We are
countrymen, you see.'

Anton Vanijek. Of course. She had seen him play
when she was thirteen years old, and had never forgotten
the magic of his artistry. Aunt Betty had never had to
push her to practise again.

'Has he been here long, Eric?'

'Too long. He. . .' The answer was lost in a deafening
crash from outside the office and several voices raised in
anger. 'Excuse me.' The OT supervisor quickly replaced
the violin in its box and left the office.

Caroline sat gazing at the soft curves of the unfinished
instrument, then carefully put back the wrapping, covering it securely and replaced the lid. Holding the box on
her lap, she was surprised to feel the slight sting of tears
in her eyes.

CHAPTER FIVE

ERIC returned after a few minutes. 'That Fred is a troublesome man. He is on your ward, Nurse?'

Caroline tried to remember the name. She thought Fred was the name of the large man who complained in the group about losing something. 'Yes, I think so. Is he a big man, with a florid complexion?'

'His face is red, yes,' Eric took the box from Caroline, 'and he is very angry right now. I sent him back to the ward. He upsets the others with his demands.'

'What was the noise?' Caroline had been too pre-occupied with her own thoughts to worry about the workroom, but the voices had sounded very angry.

'Fred pushed over a bench and upset Terry's work. Terry did not like that.' Eric was putting the violin box back on its protected shelf and replacing large cartons in front of it. 'I must return to them now, but I wished you to see. . .' He smiled at her. 'I too wish more for the Maestro—more than packing card boxes.'

'Thank you. I'm glad you showed me. It is beautiful and I know. . .well, I hope he likes it.' She could not be certain how the musician would respond. She needed to know much more about his illness and was beginning to plan how she might start, as soon as she returned to the ward.

Caroline smiled warmly at the skilled craftsman. 'May I join an activity?'

'Of course. Any you wish.' He waved an expansive hand over the room and Caroline made her way to a far wall where she saw Mr Lawrence bent over a small table spread with coloured plastic strips.

She saw he was weaving the strips into a patterned footstool and he smiled shyly as she joined him. To her surprise, she found the weaving more difficult than she had expected, as pulling the strips tightly over the small wooden frame required strong hands. Her weaving was too loose and sagged sadly.

Mr Lawrence seemed glad of her company and patiently showed her how to interweave each strip and fasten it securely. Just as she was beginning to make some progress, Caroline was surprised at the sound of a soft buzzer.

'Lunchtime.' Mr Lawrence pushed his half-finished stool under the worktable. Caroline noted it had his name on it and she placed her poor attempt beside his.

'What day is it?' Mr Lawrence stopped his movements abruptly and peered closely at Caroline's face.

'It's Monday, Mr Lawrence. Why do you ask?'

He made a slight grimace. 'Pah. Monday is always roast beef—too tough.'

'I'll come over with you.' As she offered him her arm, she accompanied his unsteady gait out of the workshop. She grinned at Eric as they left and waved at him briefly.

Back on the ward she found Ruby waiting for Mr Lawrence, with his roast beef already cut up for him. 'Why don't you go off to lunch now, Caroline? We have enough to cover the dining-room.'

'Are you sure?' Caroline wanted to take her full share in the responsibility of staffing the ward.

'Yes, we're fine. When you get back we can go over the ward procedure book and the nursing notes.' Ruby smiled and moved towards a nearby patient who had tipped over his glass of milk.

'Thanks.' As she hurried away, Caroline hoped some of her set were at their usual corner table. She was glad to see Andrew and Tracey already settled as she queued with her tray. She quickly chose an omelette and salad before making her way over to the corner. Annabelle had also arrived.

Andrew glanced up at Caroline. 'They must be joking with this. Is this really food fit for humans?'

'If you don't want it. . .' Tracey was looking hopefully at the untouched plate.

'No such luck, Tracey. I have to keep up my strength.'

'And what's this I hear about our Caroline—arriving back on Sunday morning, hmm?'

Caroline felt her cheeks flush. 'Don't be silly, Tracey.'

'Who's silly? You did!' Tracey turned to face her friend. 'And what went on between you and our handsome hero, is what I'd like to know!'

'N-nothing. Nothing went on. . .' Caroline stammered, 'I just. . .fell asleep, that's all. . .'

The entire group burst out laughing and, as she noticed some heads turn in their direction, Caroline went pink with mortification.

As Tracey and Annabelle tried to give a coherent report of Saturday night, Caroline slowly let out the deep breath she had been holding in. Andrew was going and the other girls were comparing notes on their weekend activities.

'I have to get back. See you later.' Caroline eased her way behind Tracey and, as the others cheerfully acknowledged her departure, she gratefully made her way back to the ward.

The afternoon went quickly for Caroline. Going over the ward procedure manual with Ruby gave her a sense of direction, and she then went over the Kardex, trying to put names to faces. Feeling more confident about being able to identify individual patients, she asked permission to look at some patients' medical notes.

Margaret Clarke agreed to her request and unlocked the files for Anton Vanijek and Terry Mapley. Because Caroline had already established an initial degree of rapport with these two patients, reading the confidential information was justified. The ward sister did not agree to requests to read such files merely for curiosity.

Caroline was surprised at the thinness of Terry's medical file. As she had guessed, he had been admitted several times, having slashed his arms or wrists. There were no detailed records of interviews other than a brief note by a psychologist, offering the opnion that the boy seemed to have a 'problem with authority'. Caroline wrinkled her brow. Didn't all adolescents have problems with authority? It seemed to her that this was a normal part of growing up.

She turned to the other file which was much thicker

and the information was more helpful. The violinist had not performed in public since his wife's death in a car accident five years previously. He had been out of the country at the time on a concert tour. Since then he had been re-admitted several times with a diagnosis of 'reactive depression'. Admission was required when he would stop eating for long periods, and each in-patient stay lasted between six and eight weeks.

Caroline sighed. His depression was perfectly understandable, but it seemed such a waste for a gifted man to spend the rest of his life on a treadmill of repeated admissions to a psychiatric ward. She doubted that she would be able to help him when so many others had apparently failed, but at least she now had a focus for her reading and study.

At three o'clock she watched Ruby do the drug check with the afternoon staff nurse, a large West Indian man who cheerfully introduced himself. 'Hi there. I'm Winston—welcome to the gang.'

The drug count was another familiar routine, but it would be some time before Caroline knew she could be sure of all the names for the brightly coloured tranquilliser tablets.

'Caroline, I hate to ask you, but could you do us a favour?' Ruby sighed, with a hint of exasperation. 'We haven't had the pharmacy box over yet. Charlie is supposed to bring it but he hasn't shown up. He's not very reliable, I'm afraid, and we're short of porters. Do you think you could pick it up before you go off?'

Caroline quickly agreed and, following Ruby's directions, found the hospital pharmacy department at the back of the administration building. She wondered if Charlie was the same person as the lodge porter. She could understand his reluctance to deliver the ward boxes; in winter it must be a cold job carrying pharmacy supplies to all the ward buildings. Walking up the deeply worn wooden steps into the old building, Caroline had the odd but comfortable feeling that she was following the footsteps of hundreds of people who had formed the hollows that seemed to fit her own feet so perfectly.

Smiling at her own romanticism, Caroline went

through the well-known routine of checking the contents in the familiar brown cardboard container and signing the requisition sheet before running back to the ward.

'Thanks, Caroline. There's hot coffee in our kitchen, if you want it.' Winston started to recheck the contents of the box. 'Just across the hall.'

Feeling the need to warm her slightly chilled bones, Caroline opened the door opposite the office and was delighted to see she had found the staff lockers. She could hear voices in a screened-off area at the end of the long room, beyond the well-worn easy chairs cluttered with magazines. She stopped at the open door, feeling as if she was intruding.

The group of people at the table looked so comfortable and at ease that she had the acute impression of being an outsider. David Hunter was lounging on one side of the small kitchen table, balancing precariously on a chair tipped backwards against a counter. Margaret Clarke and Jean Mansin were across the table, stirring mugs of coffee. The ward sister glanced up at the doorway.

'Good heavens, Caroline, you look frozen. Where have you been? I would have thought you would be off duty by now.'

'I went over for the pharmacy box, Sister. I didn't realise it was quite so cold.'

'That Charlie again,' Margaret Clarke muttered to herself.

'The coffee's still hot. Have a seat.' David Hunter's spontaneous smile caused a small flutter in her chest and she glanced at the chair he had pulled out next to him. Without losing his balance, she noted. She could feel her cheeks redden and hoped the others would attribute her heightened colour to the warmth of the kitchen. This man seemed to be having an unwelcome effect on her metabolism.

'Thank you.' Caroline accepted the cup offered by the Senior Tutor and sat carefully in the offered chair. At least she wouldn't have to look directly at that tanned, angular face and she smiled her gratitude as Maragaret Clarke poured her coffee. It was hot and she felt the welcome warmth spread through her. 'I don't want to interrupt your conversation.'

'Ha! Just as well. These two old fogeys are arguing with me, as usual.' David Hunter did not sound very upset at this situation.

'We never argue with you, David—merely give you the benefit of our superior experience, that's all.' Jean Mansin's eyes were twinkling. It seemed to Caroline that the tutor was enjoying her argument with the senior registrar.

'I hate to interrupt this cheerful gathering, but there are storm clouds on the horizon.' The speaker was a sturdily built woman dressed in jeans and a bright green T-shirt emblazoned with a red logo reading 'Affirmative Action'. She had come through swiftly from the locker-room and headed for the nearly empty coffee-pot.

'What's up, then, Gillian?' David Hunter looked up smilingly. 'Oh, Gillian, this is Caroline Lawson—first day today. Gillian is one of our sterling social workers.' He looked down at Caroline.

Caroline responded to the friendly nod and made room for the energetic woman at the table.

'We have yet another Section coming in and this one could be a handful.' This speech was punctuated with quick sips of coffee.

David groaned lightly and Meg sighed as she pulled her notebook out of her pocket.

'More room shuffling, I suppose?' The ward sister was looking at a list she had pulled from the small book.

'If you can. He'll probably need a single—at least until we can do the assessment.' The social worker looked over at David Hunter. 'Would tomorrow morning be OK? I can't do it tonight. Have to go to a district meeting and it's sure to drag on.'

'Fine, Gillian. I'll have a look tonight and be here again tomorrow. Around ten all right?'

'Super.' Gillian was rapidly finishing her drink.

'Any background you can give us before you dart off again?' The ward sister had produced a pen, now poised above her notes, waiting for the social worker's information.

'Not a lot.' Gillian put down her mug. 'We got a call from the police about two hours ago to the Community Services. Seems a young man was running around a local shopping mall, preaching doom and gloom at the top of his lungs.' She grinned over at Meg. 'And yours truly drew the short straw.'

'Which means us as well.' Meg smiled back at the social worker.

'Too true. Anyway, I managed to corner him, with the help of a couple of the burly boys in blue, in the back of a sweet shop.' She grinned with a mischievous glint in her eyes. 'We certainly cleared that shop in a hurry.'

Caroline was listening with open curiosity. This was another aspect of psychiatry that was new to her. She hadn't known that social workers worked with the police.

Gillian was continuing, 'I couldn't get much sense out of him. He could be paranoid, I don't know. No signs of drug taking.' She glanced at David and he nodded. 'He was going on about sin and destruction—he being the cause of catastrophe, et cetera, et cetera.'

'How old, do you think?' Meg's pen was moving steadily on the paper.

'Maybe nineteen or twenty, not much more,' Gillian answered thoughtfully. 'Very thin, possibly mal-nourished. May have been living on the streets, no identification. Says his name is Martin and won't talk about any family.' She sighed. 'So more paper shuffling and hours on the telephone. Let's hope he's a local lad.' She started to push her chair back. 'Must be off.'

'Thanks, Gill. I'll see you tomorrow.' David gave her a slight wave as he brought his chair forward with a clatter. 'Have you got a single, Meg?'

'Yes, there's one empty. I'll let Winston know.' She started to rise but was interrupted by Jean Mansin.

'I'll tell him. It's time for me to get over to Whitney anyway.'

Just as the tutor reached the outer door she could be heard cheerfully greeting someone, and Winston's head then appeared around the kitchen screen. 'Action stations, Meg?' He had raised his eyebrows in her direction.

'Possibly.' Just as she spoke, the distant wail of a police siren could be heard and she stood up quickly. 'Oh, no, they don't. They should know by now what I think of that noise!'

David Hunter laughed quietly as the ward sister quickly followed the staff nurse out to the ward. Caroline looked up at the vibrant blue eyes, now creased with amusement.

He answered the question on her face. 'Meg strongly disapproves of the dramatic entrances favoured by the local constabulary.'

'You mean the sirens?' She tried to ignore the odd effect those perceptive eyes were having on her pulse-rate.

'And the uniforms. She won't have a uniformed officer on the unit. Says it upsets the patients.' He shrugged lightly. 'And she's probably right, as usual.' He leaned forward on his elbows and looked sideways at her. 'I think we should watch this—the experts in action. Shall we?'

Caroline had moved away from his disturbing presence, but she did want to see how such patients were handled. 'Which section is he under?' Thank heavens she knew a little bit about the Mental Health Act from the 'Legal Aspects' lecture.

'Section 136. It's a bit they forgot to rewrite in the 1983 version. It's left over from the old 1959 Act. The police can ask for involuntary admission for assessment. The maximum limit is seventy-two hours.' He started to rise from the table. 'That's a long time for the patient, so Gillian and I do the assessment as soon as possible.'

He was already striding through the door leading to the ward as Caroline hurried to follow him. As they rounded the corner of the corridor leading to the main door, the ward sister's voice could be clearly heard.

'Not a step further!' Margaret Clarke was confronting two tall and very young uniformed police officers.

Caroline heard David mutter under his breath. 'New boys, about to learn Meg's rules.'

'But ma'am. . .our orders——' One officer attempted to remonstrate.

'I don't care about your orders. This is my ward and you stop right there.' The ward sister's feet were firmly planted in the centre of the corridor. Winston stood further back, leaning slightly against the wall, smiling quietly.

Caroline's eyes were drawn to the unkempt young man between the two policemen. He was very pale, dressed in frayed jeans and a dirty-looking woollen jumper. She could see he had no shoes on and his feet were blue with cold. His head was held high and his eyes were darting rapidly around at the faces surrounding him, the institutional grey walls and the glaring fluorescent ceiling lights.

She was reminded of the frantic fear in the eyes of a captured wild animal. There was a strange glitter in the young man's black eyes and the long dark hair falling half over his face only added to the impression of desperation he presented.

Caroline felt a tiny shiver run through her. She could well understand why people had believed the mentally ill to be possessed by the devil. This thin boy certainly did look as if he were possessed by something. Don't be silly, she reminded herself. He's just a disturbed boy and there must be a reason for his behaviour.

She heard the ward sister make another demand: 'Off!'

With a shock of pity, Caroline realised the boy had been handcuffed and one of the young officers was rather sheepishly unlocking the steel bracelet.

'Thank you.' Margaret Clarke dismissed the officers with a peremptory snap in her voice and took the young man firmly by the arm. 'Welcome, Martin. This is Folkestone unit and I am the ward sister. You will be with us for a few days. Will you come with me, please?'

As the boy seemed ready to jerk his arm away from the nurse's grasp, Caroline felt a sudden tenseness in the tall back of David Hunter in front of her. Yet again, she was standing slightly behind the now familiar broad shoulder and she realised he had been alert to every movement of the patient.

So this observation of the patient's arrival had not been entirely for Caroline's benefit; he had been ready to move in support of the ward sister, as had the casually leaning staff nurse who now quietly moved to follow the two back to the ward. Caroline found this knowledge strangely comforting, although she didn't know whether this was because it was good to know that the staff were mutually supportive or that this particular doctor was ready to act to protect a woman he obviously liked.

Shrugging off this thought, Caroline deliberately moved slightly away from the shelter of the shoulder beside her. At this instant the boy Martin was opposite her, still firmly in the clasp of the ward sister.

Caroline's brief movement caught his eye and she found herself staring into those fathomless black pools of fear. In the seconds that their eyes locked, she was aware of a turmoil of emotions in the boy's glance—despair, panic, desperation, and something more. Was it a plea? For help, for understanding, for rescue? She didn't know, and the boy's gaze swept away in a wild searching sweep ahead of him.

The intensity of his look had startled her and Caroline again shivered.

'Wait here a moment, I'll be right back.' Before she could move or say anything, David Hunter had rapidly disappeared back around the corner to the ward.

She stood where she was, thinking of the wild-eyed boy. Now she had another subject to read up, and she sighed. There seemed to be too much to learn.

'Here.' David Hunter had returned and placed his jacket over her shoulders. 'I've left them a PRN order. I have another chore to do before I check up on young Martin. I'll walk you back to the residence.'

'Oh, I'm all right. . .' She wasn't sure she wanted his presence quite so close, but had to admit the warmth of his heavy jacket was welcome as he opened the unit door to the cool air.

'I need to check down at the lodge, to see where our Charlie has managed to hide himself.' He was striding ahead of her with disregard of the chill wind. So, he had heard Margaret Clarke's muttered comment.

Caroline quickened her steps to catch up and tried to match his pace. 'I'm going over to the library first.'

'Fine. It's the same direction,' he replied without looking back at her.

So much for conversation with this man, she thought, and resigned herself to a very rapid walk across the hospital grounds. When they reached the school building, David Hunter paused and accepted the return of his jacket with a cheerful, 'See you tomorrow.'

He continued his loping strides in the direction of the front gates and Caroline watched him rapidly disappear around the corner of the residence. She slowly entered the empty school of nursing. The library had always been a welcome refuge with the lovely smell of old paper and slightly musty book bindings. This time she headed for the rack of new texts and magazines. Slowly the lingering image of warm blue eyes with crinkling laugh lines was replaced by a haunting memory of dark-ringed black pools in a gaunt face as she tried to make sense of the clinical descriptive terms crowding the pages in front of her.

CHAPTER SIX

FILLED with energy and determination, Caroline arrived on the ward early the following morning. The morning report included the information that the new patient had not slept and had spoken very little to the afternoon or night staff. Caroline received her patient assignments—five patients, including Terry and Mr Vanijek.

She immediately busied herself with serving breakfasts and again sat for a while with the musician, only this time she brought her own cup of tea. Again he joined her, but had eaten no breakfast. Caroline introduced herself and they sat in comfortable silence. The book had said to work slowly, so she occupied herself with thinking of ways of coaxing him to eat. If patience was needed then she would learn to wait.

After breakfast she made another round of the ward and introduced herself to her assigned patients, helping with bed-making and dressing for those who needed or wanted assistance. Looking in briefly at the open door of Martin's room, she saw him curled up on the bed with his back to the door. He had not been assigned to any one staff member until his assessment had been completed. She wondered how David Hunter would get the boy to talk to him; she had no doubt about the doctor's ability to reach through any patient's distrust.

The rest of the morning was spent in OT, sitting beside Mr Lawrence, trying to match his skill with the plastic strips. This time she watched all of the patients as unobtrusively as possible. Terry was working steadily at shaping his wooden baton; Eric had kept Fred occupied at the other end of the room. He seemed to be using some sort of leather-working tool, punching holes with vigour. Quite suitable, thought Caroline, smiling to herself. Perhaps OT activities did have some therapeutic value.

Mr Vanijek continued to calmly sort and pack his piles of cards and the still restless Bob maintained a steady hammering of nails into wooden planks. Caroline couldn't see what he was making—it didn't resemble any object she had ever seen.

During lunch she stayed with Mr Lawrence, as Ruby had the day off. The Bakewell tart was too difficult for him to eat, although she knew he would love the custard. There was always fresh fruit available, which the patients rarely touched, and she took some into the staff kitchen to cut up into small pieces. It occured to her that Mr Vanijek might be tempted with some so she sorted out a small selection. After covering Mr Lawrence's portion with custard and acknowledging his toothless grin of thanks, she quietly placed a small bowl of fruit salad in front of Mr Vanijek. She smiled, ignored his startled look and left, to return to her other patients.

As the dining-room emptied she went to clear his dishes and felt like cheering out loud. Mr Vanijek had eaten half of his fruit. Flushed with triumph, she hummed softly as she inspected the dilapidated games cupboard.

Most of the patients were in therapy groups in the early afternoon, but Mr Lawrence was excused as he usually fell asleep. The new students were not yet assigned to therapy groups and Caroline was relieved at this decision. She would be on afternoon duty next week and wouldn't be able to attend regularly for another month. She felt she had enough learning to do, without trying to understand group theories as well.

The tea-trolley had arrived and as one of the student nurses was serving, she went off to write up her nursing notes.

This was difficult to do, without the usual vital sign observations and medication records of general nursing. She was nibbling at her pen when Margaret Clarke came in to write up the ward shift report.

'Having trouble, Caroline?'

'It's just different, Sister. I don't know what is really important enough to write down.' She looked up with a slightly puzzled expression.

'Sometimes just the daily activities are important for our people. What did you do during the day?' The ward sister settled herself with her own paperwork.

Caroline outlined her own day briefly and added with a smile, 'And Mr Vanijek ate some fruit at lunch.'

'Well done, Caroline!' The older nurse turned and nodded. 'That *is* important. If he can start eating on his own, we won't have to increase his antidepressant medication. I know he dislikes it and stops taking it when he goes home—so back he comes.' She sighed.

Caroline added her observations during OT for all of her patients and handed her notes to Margaret Clarke. 'Could you look at them, please? I don't know if I've written enough.'

The experienced nurse nodded. So this was a nurse with a need to do the right thing. Psychiatric nursing might provide a few surprises for such a girl. 'These look fine, Caroline.' She handed back the notes. 'Winston should be here shortly. Could you go over the drugs with him before report, please?'

Caroline accepted the offered keys and retreated to the drug cupboard in the back alcove of the office. She could use this opportunity to learn the names and appearances of the unfamiliar psychiatric drugs.

When Winston arrived, she was concentrating on checking the bottles against the ward list. She noticed he was carrying the pharmacy box.

'No Charlie again?' she asked.

'I guess not. I just check on my way in now. It's easier than waiting to see if it arrives.' He smiled at her and they both focused their attention on double-checking the supplies before countersigning the drug sheets and joining the other staff for the shift report.

Caroline was happy to learn that Martin had agreed to stay as a voluntary patient and the Section 136 was no longer in force. David Hunter has indeed had a useful interview with the boy and had agreed with Gillian to use a working diagnosis of 'anxiety attack' for the time being. It would take time to establish if Martin was suffering from a psychotic thought disorder, and all staff were requested to keep him under close observation. He was not to leave the ward unaccompanied, and would receive no medication, although PRN sedation was available if needed.

As she made her way back to the residence, Caroline felt relaxed and exhausted.

On the Wednesday she made a discovery on the ward that added a completeness to her feeling of belonging in this new world. During her habitual tour of the ward after breakfast, she noticed the door of the empty workroom was slightly ajar. When she looked in, the large space was uninhabited and she stepped in for a closer inspection.

On the bare walls she could see marks where heavy bolts had been removed. Probably for benches like the ones in the OT building, she thought. There was a door leading off the far end of the room. This could have been the supervisor's office. She turned slowly, glancing over the stacked and scattered plastic and wooden chairs. It looked as if someone had been trying to clean; there was a broom and dustpan propped in a corner and small piles of old newspapers and debris scattered around the floor.

As she turned back towards the door, she saw the piano. It was a small upright, covered with dust and partly hidden by a stack of chairs. Caroline's spirits lifted at the sight of it and she went over to carefully move the chairs aside. The piano looked very old but sturdy enough, as she traced a pattern in the heavy dust on the closed lid.

Praying it still had keys, she carefully lifted the keyboard cover and smiled with delight as she read the flaking gold lettering. Osbert. Of course. The perfect name for a genteel Victorian gentleman. Wondering if Osbert still had a voice, she gently pressed a yellowed key and was rewarded with a faint mellow note. She patted the scratched lid with affection as she carefully closed the long-unused keyboard.

'You wait a bit longer, my old friend,' she whispered. 'Now I know you are here, I'll be back, and we'll see just how out of tune you are.'

It was not until after the end of her shift that Caroline returned to the empty room. The door was closed but unlocked, and she quickly shut it behind her. No one should hear, if she experimented quietly. She moved a small wooden chair into position and lifted the cover slowly.

The music holder seemed very fragile as she placed it in position. The music would have to come from memory and it had been a long time. Too long. She flexed her fingers; they were much too tight, but then Osbert probably wouldn't mind.

She tried a tentative arpeggio and snorted softly. Her fingers were uncoordinated and Osbert sounded badly flat. Some of the keys were sticky. She tried again. Better. Now where was that really sticky one—the A above middle C. Bother.

She became absorbed in the sounds and could feel the tension in her dormant muscles—fingers, wrists, arms, shoulders and back all ached slightly. As she began an old favourite Bach prelude, she did not hear the door open behind her. The prelude was a simple one, used by beginners, but she had always loved it. Aunt Betty would stop her work to listen and Caroline had begun and ended every practice session with the steady soothing harmonies in C major.

During her second attempt, memories of that comfortable, familiar sitting-room flooded her mind. Aunt Betty would be sitting with her workworn hands entwined in a tea-towel held absolutely still on an aproned lap, listening with a proud smile. A quiet happiness filled Caroline as she ended the music on a soft chord of reminiscence.

A slight movement behind her caused her to turn suddenly, startled. Anton Vanijek was seated on a plastic chair and she immediately felt flustered. One of the world's finest musicians had been listening to her pitiful efforts.

'Oh.' Caroline could think of nothing to say.

The quiet grey eyes looked at her solemnly and Anton Vanijek nodded slowly. 'I like Bach. Like heartbeats.'

Caroline's mind was moving swiftly. Perhaps she could use music to reach out to this man. He was at least talking to her. She racked her brain trying to think of violin and piano sonatas. They would all be difficult, but she might try.

'Do you know the C minor prelude?' His voice was low and the words came slowly.

'I. . . I don't know. Which one?' She tried to remember all the Bach preludes; there were so many.

'It is BWV 999.' He smiled briefly. 'A useful number—I remember it.'

Caroline returned his smile. The one number every person in the country knew—at least she would be able to find the music. She knew this was music she would find and learn to play to perfection, if this man asked to hear it.

She shook her head, still doubtful of which prelude he meant.

'May I?' He pointed to the keyboard.

'Of course.' Caroline carefully kept the excitement out of her voice. She moved away and left the chair for him, watching with a sense of awe as he bent over the keyboard.

Very slowly and with precision, the long, slender fingers depressed the keys. She heard him mutter to himself 'semi-tone flat' but the harmony was recognisable.

'Yes?' His fingers stopped and he looked up at her.

'Yes, I remember. But not very well, I'm afraid.' She took the chair he had vacated and paused. She felt embarrassed to play before this man and took a deep breath. Just pretend it's Aunt Betty sitting there. The key of C minor had always seemed so tragic and dark. Perhaps that was why he wanted to hear it.

She started tentatively but her memory held and the intricate harmonies fell into place. The sticky A natural caused an uneven break in the rhythm, but she could feel her fingers beginning to flow more easily and she played the slow arpeggio at the end as a peaceful close.

As she turned with an apologetic smile, Anton Vanijek nodded. 'Thank you.' He again looked at her solemnly. 'Bach speaks to the heart.' He started to rise. 'May I listen again?'

'If you wish. It would be my pleasure, Mr Vanijek.' Caroline gave an inward sigh. Now she had to find a Bach album and practise. The textbooks hadn't mentioned this, but then theories could hardly apply to every specific patient. If this patient wanted to hear Bach, then that was what she would play. She closed up the piano with a final pat of satisfaction, Osbert might just prove to be the best therapist of them all.

As she left and closed the door, a heavy thud was heard from the slightly open door in the disused office at the far end of the room. David Hunter picked himself up off the dusty floor and rubbed his bruised knee roughly.

'Damn!' A deep muttered exclamation accompanied the slight creak as he straightened his stiff leg. 'Next time, old man, find a better seat than a dodgy three-legged stool.' He started to pick up some loose papers and looked around for his pen.

'One more item to add to the list. Now where does one find a piano tuner in these parts?' He scribbled briefly on his pad and smiled thoughtfully. 'It seems the sparrow can sing, and very beautifully at that.' He wondered if the entertainment budget would stretch to the hiring of a grand piano, but shrugged off the thought. No sense in reaching for the moon; sparrows lived closer to the earth. As he closed up the office he heard himself whistling Bach. So it was the classics, was it? Another idea began to glimmer at the back of his mind and he whistled more loudly as he left the ward to keep his appointment with Eric.

Caroline arrived early for the Thursday morning ward meeting and carefully chose a seat opposite the vacant armchair. She was not going to shelter behind the broad shoulder this time, and the fact that she could see Dr Hunter clearly from across the room was of no relevance whatsoever. As the room filled and the chairs behind David Hunter remained empty, she wondered where Terry was.

Her thoughts were interrupted by the deep voice of David Hunter breaking into the silence.

'There is something I would like to discuss with the group.' He was smiling calmly at all the suddenly expectant faces. 'We have opened the empty room at the end of the unit and I was thinking we could use it for. . .perhaps entertainment purposes.'

'What do you mean—entertainment?' Even a normal question from Fred sounded belligerent.

'We might use it as a music-room.' David's hand moved in a slow arc to indicate the empty chair behind him. 'Terry has managed to get some of the drums from the village and there's an old piano in there.' His bland smile covered them all, but it seemed to Caroline that his eyes twinkled as he glanced at her before turning away.

A sudden suspicion shot through her mind. He couldn't know she had played that piano, could he? She wouldn't put it past him. Now she supposed she would have to accompany group sing-songs. Hallelujah, she thought morosely. Still, that might not be so bad if David Hunter wanted to sing.

Setting off for OT with Mr Lawrence, she passed an ancient van rumbling up to Folkestone, driven by a grinning Terry. He waved at her and, as she returned the greeting, she was reminded of the speed with which a certain doctor managed to get things moving. It seemed the drums had arrived.

In OT she found Eric busily sorting out long planks of wood and writing out detailed instructions for an attentive Bob. The supervisor smiled broadly at Caroline's questioning glance.

'For Folkestone. Dr Hunter wants a platform, with steps.' He nodded with satisfaction. 'This is a good job for carpentry. It is good to have a purpose for work.'

Caroline murmured agreement and took up her plastic weaving thoughtfully. Just what was David Hunter planning? He seemed to involve everyone in his schemes. Now Bob could happily hammer nails indefinitely and she winced slightly as the raucous sound of an electric saw started up at the end of the room.

She had not returned to the piano during the rest of the week, but was preoccupied with the problem of finding the music she needed. If she took an early train on Saturday she could visit Aunt Betty and then stop in a favourite music shop in the West End where the staff had always been helpful. The problem was the irregularity of the local bus service. She was telephoning for the train schedule from the call box in the lounge when Tracey and Annabelle burst in, on the Friday afternoon.

'Caroline, where have you been?' Tracey looked as if she would explode with excitement.

'Come out here! You won't believe it!' Annabelle tugged at Caroline's arm impatiently.

'What?' She found herself being pulled away, so she hung up the telephone and allowed herself to be propelled along the corridor towards the outside door.

'Come on!' Tracey was running to open the door and Annabelle pushed Caroline to the top of the outside steps. 'Look!'

Propped up against the lowest steps, embellished with a gigantic scarlet bow, was a freshly painted, very old blue bicycle.

'See. . .it's for you!' Tracey waved the large hand-lettered card with 'Caroline Lawson' printed in large black letters.

As Caroline stared in delighted disbelief, Annabelle was burbling, 'Who's it from, Caroline? Who sent it? I didn't know you wanted a bicycle!' Her words were tumbling over each other.

Caroline laughed out loud as she reached down to ring the silver bell. That man was unbelievable. He had actually painted the old bicycle blue. Surely he couldn't mean her to have it? She certainly couldn't keep it, but she felt a surge of gratitude to David Hunter for his generous gesture. Now she could get to the train station without waiting for the bus.

She touched the royal-blue frame. The colour was not precisely the shade of those clear, vivid eyes, but it was certainly blue.

Caroline's heart was light as she planned her weekend. A quick ride into the village to purchase a chain and padlock was exhilarating and she discovered a deserted side-road that provided an easy, level ride back to the hospital. She had forgotten the delicious feeling of freedom when riding alone and again she whispered a silent thanks to David Hunter. She really must find a way to thank him, but that would require some careful thought.

Saturday morning was clear; the pale sunlight filtering through the soft air touched the countryside with a delicate filminess. Caroline squinted her eyes slightly. It was like looking at the world through an old dusty mirror—images were faint and slightly blurred. Soon the days would lengthen and the light would sharpen the edges, but she liked the haziness. Like antique lace, she thought, to be touched gently, taking care not to tear the finely woven threads.

She was humming lightly as she fastened the bicycle securely outside the train station and was surprised to see Alison climbing out of the Range Rover.

'Hi. Going up to London?' Caroline would be glad of

company. The ride could seem long, especially when she was in a hurry.

Alison joined her and they chatted easily during the journey. Alison seemed reluctant to explain precisely what she planned to do in the city. 'Just shopping' was her answer to Caroline's question. She entertained them both with stories of the activities on the children's ward and Caroline was happy to hear how much Alison was enjoying her experience. Sometimes she had wondered how the apparently light-hearted girl would respond to the difficulties of working with emotionally disturbed people but it seemed Alison was flourishing at Castleview.

They parted in London; Alison to flag down a taxi and Caroline to head for the Underground. She thought it would be faster and she had a lot to do. The visit with Aunt Betty followed the usual routine, and Caroline felt slightly despondent after the half-hour of one-sided conversation. Every time she visited, she had a secret hope that Aunt Betty would respond in some way. But no, even the mention of a blue bicycle had evoked no visible reaction from the immobile face. Merely a brief opening of the eyes when she arrived and nothing more.

With a sigh, Caroline chose an Underground route to get to the music store. Her mood darkened as the train unexpectedly stopped in a tunnel. As the minutes ticked by, she could feel her impatience rising. It was the sense of powerlessness she hated most, and she hadn't thought to bring a book to read. She looked at her watch. She would be cutting it fine if the train didn't move soon, and she fretted at her enforced immobility.

After finally making her connection and racing to the shop, she found she was too late. It had closed, and she felt like stamping her foot in frustration. A childlike temper tantrum would have felt most satisfying. Nothing was going the way she had planned, and she slowly made her way back, catching a late train. There was no sign of Alison or her Range Rover when Caroline finally unchained the bicycle for her ride to the hospital.

She awoke early on Sunday with an idea. She could go to the church in the village. Surely churches had Bach music—probably organ fugues, but better than nothing. She dressed quickly and had an impromptu cheese breakfast in the residence kitchen.

Recovering the bicycle from its protected spot under the stairwell, she took off with renewed hope. The day was an overcast grey and she tried to remember where the sound of church bells had come from. Stupid not to have asked at the village shop yesterday. Well, she hadn't thought of it then, had she?

She finally found the small stone church and it was clearly locked. There was no sign of occupancy and she looked at her watch. Nine-thirty. Again, she was too late. Hadn't David Hunter said the service was at eight-thirty? She looked at the bolted door with disappointment. It looked a very pretty church and she would have liked to see inside.

This weekend had not turned into one of her most successful. Next weekend she would be on duty and she was determined to make good use of the remaining free time. No more wild-goose chases.

Caroline buckled down to study for the rest of the day.

Monday was Caroline's first time on the afternoon shift and she found the evening hours much more relaxed than the busier day schedule. Very few of the patients had visitors and the use of the extra room for activities seemed to be a good idea.

She brought Mr Lawrence and a few of the more elderly patients down, sat them on chairs and started to play a few old dance tunes. Soon they were asking for their favourites and tapping their feet. Caroline was pleased with their reaction; it was probably more meaningful to them than watching television. They were interrupted when Winston called them out for evening drinks and Caroline wandered into the staff kitchen.

If she could find some implement with which to beat time, she might be able to get some of the patients to actually sing. She looked in some of the cupboards but found nothing useful. Opening a small drawer, she found some odd bits of cutlery. She tapped a few spoons together and smiled. Terry would probably have more success with these. She picked up a large wooden spoon. Now, this was more like it. She hit it lightly on the counter. Yes, that had a good clear thump.

'Help.' A hoarse voice made her turn swiftly. Martin was standing just inside the kitchen area and staring at her.

'Oh, you startled me. Hello, Martin.' She had seen the boy wandering around the ward and there had usually been a male staff member in proximity. He had been having daily interviews with David Hunter every afternoon, but she knew a definite diagnosis had not yet been made.

'Help.' The word was spoken with more intensity and Caroline wondered where Winston was. Don't be silly, she told herself. This boy is a patient and you are a nurse.

'What are you asking for, Martin? I don't understand you.' The books said to keep your voice calm and clear, and she hoped that was what she was doing. She didn't feel the least bit calm.

Martin moved forward and put out an open hand. 'Help!'

Caroline forced herself to stand perfectly still. 'I would like to help you, Martin. Can you tell me what you want me to do?'

The black eyes were wide and staring. He took another step forward and Caroline involuntarily gripped the spoon in her hand. She could feel the old fluttering deep inside her and tried to take a deep breath.

Suddenly, with the swiftness of light, the boy's hand reached out and grabbed her sleeve. 'Help!'

'No!' Caroline moved back quickly and she heard a ripping noise. The ragged sound and the desperation in the black eyes fastened on her face fused into a cloud of grey mist and she could feel the fluttering become an overwhelming tide of choking panic. She couldn't breathe. He was too close and she had to get away. Get away from the hands. Away from the eyes. Those eyes that were gleaming like black embers. They would burn. They would hurt.

Through the ghostly mist she saw a gigantic hand reaching for her and she swivelled suddenly. There was another harsh tearing sound and in the far-off distance she heard a long, high scream of terror. She swung with all her strength and struck out blindly.

The hand and eyes disappeared as the grey haze closed in around her and she was safe. She was tightly enclosed within strong walls and she could rest. Gratefully she leaned her head against the solidity close to her cheek and let the tears of relief flow freely. She didn't have to fight any more.

CHAPTER SEVEN

DAVID HUNTER held the shuddering softness of Caroline close to his heart. Her scream had pierced him in the depths of his being and he knew he had never moved so fast in his life. The look of naked fear on her face as she raised her hand to defend herself would be engraved forever in his memory.

As he softly stroked the dark head buried in his shoulder, he nodded to Winston as the nurse led Martin back to his room. The boy would have a sore ear for a day or so, but David's worry was for the girl he cradled tightly in his arms. He could feel the smooth roundness of her breast pressed against his chest and her slowly subsiding shivering spasms echoed his own pounding heartbeats.

He murmured into the ear beneath his hands, 'Quietly, Caro, quietly. Nothing bad will happen. Nothing will hurt you.'

He could hear the choking sobs and her gulping efforts to catch her breath. He continued his murmurings and could feel the beginnings of a deep, dark rage start within him. This was an old anger he had thought long dead. He could feel his hands starting to shake as he brushed the curve of her arm curled against him. There were the beginnings of a discoloured bruise where the boy had grabbed her arm, and David deliberately continued to talk in a low, quiet voice as much to himself as to calm the girl.

'Nothing bad. . .no more hurt. No more pain. . .no more hurting.' He looked up to see Meg Clarke with Jean Mansin behind her. Good for Winston; he could be relied on to call on the needed supports.

Meg had taken off her cardigan and placed it around Caroline's bare shoulder. 'It's all right, David. We'll take her now.'

She gently put her arms around Caroline and slowly withdrew her from David's clasp. He gave her up reluctantly and tried to steady his own trembling.

Meg looked up at him. 'Put on the coffee-pot, I'll be right back.' She led Caroline out of the kitchen towards the ward office, with the tutor right behind them.

The ward sister returned within minutes to see David slumped over the kitchen table, staring unseeingly at a blank wall. He looked up as she came in.

'What can I do?' His voice was harsh and she could hear the bitterness with an underlying rage.

'You do nothing, David. At least for the time being.' Her voice was quiet. 'This is nursing work.' She made a mug of coffee and put it in front of him. 'I can't know exactly how you feel, but I can guess.'

'I doubt it.' He looked blankly at the mug.

'I have a suspicion how you feel about this particular nurse.' She sat down heavily. 'But as I say, for the time being, you will have to leave her to us. We can help in a way you can't—at least not yet. Perhaps later you can.'

'What do you mean, Meg? What are you talking about?' He lifted his head to look at her.

'It's difficult to explain, David.' She remained silent for a few moments. 'It's a difference between nursing and doctoring, at least in psychiatry.' She looked up at him seriously. 'I've never tried to explain it before, at least to a very young doctor.' She smiled at his flash of irritation. 'You are young, David, and relatively new to this field. So is Caroline, but she will follow in our footsteps and she is beginning to know that. You, at least professionally, will follow other paths. Medical history is different.'

David tried to concentrate on what she was saying, even though he didn't see what it had to do with his anger. 'OK, Meg, I'm listening.'

'Part of the tradition is to get grabbed, sometimes punched and always frightened by unforeseen attacks.' She looked over at his surprised face. 'Oh, yes, David, we've all been through it. Any nurse still in the field after the age of thirty has the bruises to prove it.' She gave a sad smile. 'It has nothing to do with being a bad nurse—often quite the contrary. It often seems to be the good ones that get bashed. Maybe the good ones care too much and get too close, I don't know. But that's the way it is.' She took a long drink of coffee. 'And now is the time for Caroline to know that she has joined a select group of people. It's up to us to let her know that.' She sighed again.

David interrupted, 'Not every nurse who gets hit is a mini Florence Nightingale.'

Meg nodded. 'I know. We have bad apples, like everywhere else, and we try to teach them. That's a professional duty. We can get hit, but revenge is not allowed.' She looked directly at him. 'And that goes for every other professional in the immediate vicinity as well.'

'I'd love to kick his head in, Meg, but I won't.' David tried to smile at her, but he knew it was forced.

'I know what you feel like doing. But we'll all work with this boy and we'll bend over backwards to help straighten out his confused thinking. We've done it before and we'll do it again.' She paused. 'But that isn't the immediate problem. We have Caroline, wondering what she did wrong. She did nothing wrong, and that's what we have to get her to believe.'

'True. That's obvious.'

'I think there may be more here, though.' Meg looked at him intently. 'There are deeper fears in this girl and they've probably surfaced a bit earlier that she expected.' She looked away and focused her gaze outside the window. 'The reasons for coming into psychiatry are as varied as the people who do it. We all have questions that want answering. Most of us learn to ask the right questions, eventually.' Again she paused, thoughtfully. 'I think Caroline hasn't found those right questions yet. But she's looking. And when she finds them. . .' she looked over at David's intent face '. . .it would be good to have a friend who can help her deal with the answers.'

'Yes.' His voice was low. 'We all have questions. Sometimes the answers aren't so easy.'

They sat in silence, each preoccupied with different thoughts. Finally, Margaret Clarke sighed and started to get up. 'Back to the grind, I'm afraid.'

David looked up glumly. 'Where is she now?'

'Jean took her over to the residence. I'll go over later and see how she's getting on.' She smiled sadly down at his strained face. 'You, my dear David, must stay away for a while. Let her come to you, in her own time. When she's ready to share, she will.'

He nodded slowly. 'I'm not in the habit of skulking around nurses' residences, Meg. But I get your point.' He let out a soft sigh. 'It's just hard—waiting and watching someone. . .suffer.'

She laid a hand briefly on his hunched shoulder, put her empty mug in the sink and left him alone with his thoughts.

Jean Mansin watched Caroline's face carefully. The tears had dried and she could see the beginnings of relaxing exhaustion easing the tension of the girl curled up on her bed. The teacher sat silently, waiting.

'I feel so silly, Miss Mansin.' Caroline looked over at the quiet, understanding face watching her. 'I don't usually behave quite so hysterically. It wasn't his fault.'

'No one's at fault, Caroline.' The older nurse immediately took the opportunity to reassure. 'Not only are you not silly, you handled yourself well.'

'Well?' A hoarse croak of mirthless laughter greeted this comment. 'Fighting with a patient is hardly therapeutic!'

'That depends on what you mean by therapeutic.' Jean Mansin remained calm. 'Fighting can be a normal and expected response when being attacked. None of us is superhuman, you know.'

'Well, you wouldn't have fought him. You would have known what to do!' Caroline's voice held a hint of frustration. 'How long does it take to learn the right way?'

'Some people never learn. However, you are not quite correct when you say I wouldn't fight.'

Caroline's eyes widened as she looked over at the senior tutor.

'You have no way of knowing what I would do, Caroline.' The calm voice continued and warmed, 'I've had a few good set-tos in my day, I can tell you!'

'You?' Caroline moved up on her elbows, astonished. This controlled, knowledgeable nurse had actually fought with patients? She didn't believe it.

Caroline sat up on the edge of her bed and looked carefully at the older nurse's smiling face. Taking a deep breath, she asked a question that was burning inside her.

'Miss Mansin. . .were you ever afraid?'

The smiling eyes looked at the anxious face before her, fully aware of the importance of her answer. 'Of course, Caroline. We are all afraid at some time. You would have to be senseless not to be frightened of the unknown.'

'Thank you, Miss Mansin. I feel all right now.' She smiled at the teacher and received a slight tilt of head and a friendly smile in response. 'You know the case study assignment due at the end of the month? Do you think I could do one on Martin?' She watched the tutor's face carefully.

After a pause Jean Mansin said thoughtfully, 'I hadn't thought of that, but I don't see why not.' She looked at Caroline. 'He chose you as a target for his feelings. Perhaps it is appropriate that you choose him as a focus for your learning.'

She nodded at her student, satisfied that this particular nurse was already prepared to accept the challenges and opportunities presented by the unexpected behaviours of psychiatric patients.

* * *

After report the following day, Caroline asked to talk with Margaret Clarke and asked if she could work with Martin. 'He was asking me for help and I would like to try.'

'Yes, I can understand that. May I make a few suggestions?' Meg was pleased to have her initial judgement confirmed. Caroline was willing to meet a personally difficult situation and use it to develop professional skills. The ward sister looked forward to watching and supporting this fledgling psychiatric nurse. 'You could start by sitting with him for a short period during the teatime in the lounge.'

Caroline nodded. She would be more comfortable in an open space. Part of her fear had come from having her exit blocked.

Meg Clarke continued, 'He has his daily session with David just before tea and he needs to be kept from retreating into solitude. Perhaps you can talk with David about his interviews and co-ordinate your approach with his.'

Caroline remained silent but listened carefully. She wasn't certain what she could say to the man who had offered her comfort when she had been so upset. Her recollection was a bit unclear, but she knew she probably owed him an explanation and she didn't really have one.

The ward sister's ideas were very sensible and Caroline followed the valued advice. She approached the boy quietly in the day-room that afternoon.

'Would you like a cup of tea, Martin?' she asked him quietly, and accepted his dark gaze without comment. Interpreting his silence as agreement—at least he hadn't refused—she brought two cups and sat down in a chair beside him. He took the cup and drank it down quickly.

Caroline was glad to see Winston settle himself beside Fred across the room. He was obviously keeping an unobtrusive watch on Martin, and Caroline relaxed slightly. She sipped her tea in silence while Martin folded his arms across his chest and kept his eyes downcast, looking at his feet. Caroline noticed he was now wearing hospital slippers.

As she casually watched the other patients, she was

startled to see David Hunter stride across to the tea-
trolley, help himself to a cup of tea and glance casually
over at her sitting beside Martin. She smiled tentatively
at him and he gave her a cool, friendly nod as he left the
room.

David breathed a silent sigh of relief. Meg had said he
should stay away, but he had needed to at least see
Caroline. She had looked pale but composed and
obviously in control. He was satisfied for the time being.
He trusted Meg to know what she was doing and there
was no reason why he couldn't find the time to spend a
few evening hours on Folkestone. There was always
paperwork to do, after all.

The afternoon and evening routine continued peacefully
throughout the rest of the week. Caroline's sing-song
hour after the evening meal became a regular event. She
discovered that most of the patients enjoyed old familiar
tunes and the favourite was 'It's a Long Way to
Tipperary' which Mr Lawrence sang loudly off-key with
great gusto.

Occasionally Terry would join in with a marching beat
on a small drum, and even Mr Vanijek joined the group,
although Caroline noticed he did not join in the singing.
An old song book borrowed from Whitney provided the
music for her, but it was certainly far from the Bach she
had planned.

She continued to spend time with Martin and they
both became accustomed to drinking their tea seated in
the same chairs side by side. Once, Martin wandered
into the music-room and watched for a while before
leaving as silently as he had come. Since he had not
spoken to her again, Caroline had not expected him to
join in the raucous noise the growing numbers of men
produced. The sounds might be rough, but the volume
was considerable.

David Hunter also put in brief appearances on the
edge of the group around the piano. Once he joined
Terry on the drums to provide a strong pounding rhythm
backing to a loud rendition of 'Oh, Dear, What Can the
Matter Be?' He gave an exaggerated bow to the ragged

applause of the patients and grinned at Caroline's
bemused expression. His cheerful shrug made her laugh.
It was impossible to resist his easy good humour. She
did wish he would sing; the men might be encouraged to
a closer harmony. Still, they were enjoying themselves
and she shouldn't ask any more of them.

The plan to find music for Anton Vanijek had not
been forgotten, and Caroline planned to visit the village
church again—this time earlier—to speak with the vicar.
She had been out cycling every day, learning the country
roads around the hospital. It was good to be alone with
time to think, and she always felt more relaxed before
going on to the ward in the afternoon.

The rain on Saturday morning provided as good a
reason as any to start on some overdue laundry. The
sound of raised voices from the lounge caught Caroline's
attention on the way to the washing-machine next to the
kitchen.

'What difference does it make?' The voice belonged to
Alison and she sounded very angry.

'Quite a lot, girl. You can't do it!'

Caroline stopped abruptly. She had never heard
Andrew's voice raised in anger and he was almost
shouting at Alison.

'Why not? Nobody cares!' Alison sounded close to
tears.

'You're wrong. I care.' Andrew's voice was quieter.

Caroline paused by the open door. She didn't like to
think of the high-spirited Alison in such distress, but if
it was a private argument she shouldn't intrude. Suddenly the door was pulled further open and she could see
Andrew's back as he addressed the space in front of him.
'You're heading for trouble, Alison, but if you can't see
it. . .'

He turned and saw Caroline. 'Good, you can tell her,
Caroline.' He pulled Caroline into the lounge, ignoring
her arms full of laundry. 'Come in and see what Alison's
up to.'

She looked in to see Alison seated in the midst of a
dozen opened parcels. Spread over the settee were several
items of clothing. Caroline could see they were all for

children and looked very expensive. This must have been Alison's shopping of the previous week.

'I just wanted to show Andrew.' Alison looked up at Caroline. 'I thought he would understand, but I was wrong.' She started to fold up a tiny white shirt.

'By understand, you mean agree with you, and I don't.' Andrew turned to a puzzled Caroline. 'It seems she's in love with a person who is all of five years old! Tell her she can't give all this to one kid!' He sounded very serious and Caroline looked at Alison's lowered head.

'Alison,' she sat down carefully, 'why did you want to do this? They are lovely but. . .has he no clothing?'

'They're all grotty!' Alison looked at Caroline with a pleading in her eyes. 'No one cares about him. And he really is beautiful, Caroline, really he is. He's very tiny, with the most enormous blue eyes.'

'Yes, but. . .' Caroline could understand the attraction of blue eyes, but any child could be beautiful.

'Why is he in hospital, Alison?' Andrew spoke in his normal calm voice and sat down across from the two girls.

'He eats dirt,' Alison answered.

'Dirt?' Caroline thought all children would eat dirt if they had the chance.

'All *kinds* of dirt.' Alison grinned wickedly.

'Oh.' Realisation hit Caroline.

'So? That doesn't make him clinically disturbed.' Andrew's knowledge of paediatrics was broader than theirs. 'Where is his family? His mother?'

Alison's hand struck the top of a cardboard box fiercely. 'They don't care! His mother tried to top herself—she's got six others—and can't cope.'

'Is she in hospital, too?' asked Caroline.

'I think so. Somewhere else.' Alison looked at them. 'So, you see, there's no one to take care of him.'

'Except you, you think.' Andrew nodded, as if to himself. He spoke carefully. 'Alison, you are a nurse—one of many—who cares for this boy—Ben, is it? He doesn't belong to you.'

'But nobody else cares as much as I do!' There was an edge of desperation in her voice.

Andrew sighed. Caroline thought she could understand Alison's need to offer something special; her own hunt for specific music to please an individual patient was not so very different.

'Could you give him just one of these. . .?' She lifted a small blue cardigan.

'I suppose.' Alison sounded sulky.

'Can't you see why you shouldn't give it all to one child?' Andrew's question was spoken with intensity, as if willing her to understand.

'No! No, I can't.' Alison had replaced the small articles back in their boxes and stood up, clutching the bulky bundle. 'And I don't really care what you two think.' She left in a flurry of rustling tissue paper and packages.

Andrew smiled sadly at Caroline. 'She's got so much caring in her, but how do we tell her not to give all her love to just one poor disturbed boy?'

Caroline shook her head. 'I don't know, Andrew. Is what she's doing all that wrong? She's so soft-hearted.'

'Yes, it's wrong. Very wrong. Especially for someone like Alison.' He stood up slowly. 'She's always had whatever she's wanted, but not this time.' As he helped Caroline with her laundry bag, he added, 'Nursing these people can hurt, if we're not careful. . .even the kiddies. Maybe more so with the kids, and I'm afraid Alison is headed for some painful learning.'

As she started on her washing, Caroline thought about Andrew's words. She thought she might be beginning to understand what he meant.

She was still thinking of Alison's need to give to a special child as she headed out to find the village church early the next morning. The rain had left a fresh, sparkling dew and she could smell the first slight stirrings of the reawakening earth.

This time she found the church in time, as the service had just begun. She propped the bicycle outside, near the few cars parked in the yard. She entered quietly and sat in a rear pew. The church was barely half full—the service was simple and consisted mainly of hymn singing and a brief talk by the vicar, who mentioned their hopefulness for good weather to help the spring planting.

Caroline felt she should at least join in with the singing, and she noticed a small electronic organ being energetically played by a thin, bearded man dressed in a shiny blue suit. As the few parishoners filed out after the service, talking quietly with each other, she was astonished to see the vicar unplug the organ and carry it, with the young man holding up one end, down the aisle to where she was waiting at the door.

The two men put the instrument in the back of a battered estate wagon before the vicar returned to greet his congregation.

He smiled at Caroline. 'It's good to hear a new voice.'

She returned his smile and wondered how she could ask her question, as she turned to shake another hand held out to him. She waited and watched his face. This middle-aged man with round pink cheeks and twinkling grey eyes seemed to be treated as a trusted friend.

'Vicar, I wonder. . .' She was hesitant.

'Yes, my dear? What can I do for you?' His smile was warm and patient.

Caroline introduced herself and explained her request. 'It's for a particular patient, really. He would like to hear Bach but I need some music.'

He nodded quickly. 'Yes, indeed. Well, we must certainly see what we can do. You come with me, my dear.'

He motioned her to follow him as he walked with quick steps towards his car where the thin young man sat, patiently waiting to drive them on to the next service.

'We're a bit of a travelling road show, you see. . .' He had the car door open for her and she motioned to her bicycle. 'Ah. Can you follow us, then?'

She nodded as he settled himself beside his young driver. 'We'll pass my house on the way. I'm sure we'll have something there for you.'

Caroline ran to the bicycle and set off in the wake of

Reader Service
FREEPOST
P.O. Box 236
Croydon
Surrey CR9 9EL

Send NO money now

Free Books & Gifts claim

	Free Teddy	Surprise Mystery Gift

Yes Please send me Free and without obligation Teddy and Mystery Gift. Please also reserve a subscription to your Reader Service which means I can go on to enjoy 6 Brand New Romances sent to me every month for £8.70, post and packing FREE, plus all the benefits overleaf. If I decide not to subscribe I shall write to you within 10 days. I understand that I may cancel or suspend my subscription at any time simply by writing to you.

7AOR

Mrs/Miss/Mr _____

Address _____

_____ Postcode _____

Signature _____

The right is reserved to refuse an application and change the terms of this offer. You may be mailed with other offers as a result of this application. If you would prefer not to share in this opportunity please tick box. ☐

Overseas please send for details. Readers in Southern Africa write to Independent Book Services Pty. Postbag X3010 Randburg 2125. South Africa.

mps MAILING PREFERENCE SERVICE

the rattling estate wagon. She wondered how the electronic instrument survived such rough treatment every week, but forgot that concern as she tried to keep the old vehicle in sight as they twisted through narrow country lanes.

The car slowed outside a small farmhouse and she rode up to the passenger side as the vicar waved at her. 'Just go in and ask my wife. Tell her what you need—we're bound to have it somewhere. God bless!' With that cheery benediction, he disappeared in a cloud of soft dust as the car spurted forward and proceeded on its noisy way.

Caroline sighed and looked at the house in front of her. She had come this far, she might as well carry on. Besides, she had no idea where she was and would have to ask directions back to the hospital.

As she pushed carefully up the gravel path, she could see children's toys scattered among the still empty flower-beds near the house. She bent down to inspect a particular patch. There were barely perceptible triangles of pale green starting to appear. Surely it was too early for a crocus to come; she wondered what colour they were. The sight of new growth always filled her with an impatient anticipation.

'Good morning.' A cheerful voice interrupted her thoughts. 'They're lovely when they come up. Such a sign of hope, don't you think?' A small round woman in a flowered dress was inspecting the ground carefully.

'What colour are they?' Somehow the question didn't sound as foolish as it might have, with another person.

'We're never quite sure. They're mixed and it's always a lovely surprise.' A soft laugh accompanied the answer as the little woman held out her hand to Caroline. 'I'm Mrs Wenham.'

Caroline introduced herself and again explained her request. She was bustled into the house and found herself the object of fascinated interest for two small girls as she sat in an overstuffed armchair while the vicar's wife lifted the lid of an old piano seat.

'We must have some Bach. We have everything else.' She talked happily to herself as she ruffled through old, tattered sheet music and books. 'Ah. . .' She pulled out a well-thumbed book. 'Here we are. My eldest, Ralph, used to try it,' she shook her head with a short laugh, 'but he never did like to practise. He's studying theology now.'

She handed the book to Caroline and waved away her thanks. 'You are welcome to it, my dear. We have no use for it, and there's plenty more here if these two ever show an interest.' She scooped up the two girls as she accompanied Caroline to the door.

'I'm very grateful, and I'm sure the patient will be, as well.' Caroline clutched the precious book to her. At least she had Mr Vanijek's music. 'Could you tell me how to get back to the hospital?'

Mrs Wenham's instructions were a bit confusing, but, as the pale sun was now clearly over the trees, Caroline thought she could get back by following a general northwesterly path. Holding the music book was a problem, and she tucked it securely under her pullover and tightly buttoned her jacket over it.

She pedalled slowly through the peaceful countryside, trying to keep heading in the approximate direction of the hospital. This wasn't easy as the frequent twists in the road kept turning her around. She pushed the bicycle to the top of a low rise and looked around.

Her eyes were caught and held by the distant movement of a yellow dot. It had to be. There was no other bright colour in the landscape, and who else would wear such an improbable shade of yellow? If she took the left turning, she could cross his path.

At least he can tell me how to get home, she muttered to herself, as she coasted down the side of the incline. She pedalled quickly and paused at the crossroads as the yellow jersey came closer.

David had seen the blue bicycle at the top of the hill and moderated his strides slightly to allow her time to reach the crossing before him. 'Please wait, Caro,' he breathed deeply as he ran. 'You just wait there. Please don't run. Please wait.'

As he approached her, he ran steadily, waved casually

and called out 'Coffee', pointing ahead, and ran on without stopping.

When he heard the slight squeak and rattle of the old bicycle turning to follow him, he felt his muscles ease and his breathing deepened. He loped smoothly up the drive to the house and waved her around to the kitchen entrance.

Caroline watched him disappear behind the kitchen door and placed the bicycle carefully against the decorative garage. It still looked as improbable as it first had and she smiled.

She was still smiling as she walked into the kitchen, already expecting the remembered aroma of his coffee, and she stopped up short when she saw him staring at her with a deep frown on his face.

'What's wrong?' She had never seen him frown, and his eyes had deepened to a dark ultramarine.

'What on earth have you got on?' His voice sounded astonished.

'Nothing.' She looked down at her coat and suddenly giggled. 'Oh, you mean this. . .' She opened her jacket and, feeling suddenly self-conscious, pulled the object from underneath her jumper. 'It's the music book. For Mr Vanijek. I got it from the vicar—or his wife, really.'

She could hear herself babbling as she saw his eyes warm, looking at her. She felt slightly uncomfortable and she had a vague memory of his closeness against her body. She flushed and held the book against her waist.

'Well, that's a relief. I thought you had taken to wearing a steel corset.' He turned back to the coffee-pot. 'I'm having some eggs and toast. Want some?'

'All right.' She remembered a previous breakfast in this large, warm kitchen. 'Please. If it's not too much trouble.'

He smiled softly. Too much trouble? He would build a palace of pure gold single-handed if this sparrow said she wanted one. Let's hope she doesn't, old man, he thought. You can't afford it. He whistled softly as he prepared breakfast.

She sat in comfortable silence, watching him work efficiently and with calm certainty. Who says men can't cook? she thought. It would be good to feed him, though. She looked at the height of the fair head shining in the reflection of the mid-morning sun. He must eat a great deal; there's so much of him.

Caroline brushed such thinking aside. This was his kitchen, or rather Henry's. Speaking of that lady. . .

'Is Henry here?' Her voice was carefully casual.

'No.' His back remained to her. 'She's staying with friends in Gloucestershire.'

'Oh.' That meant the house was empty. Before she could consider the implications of this information, she found a full plate of eggs, tomato and toast placed in front of her.

They ate in silence and David finished first with a satisfied languid stretch. 'Much better. Now to the task at hand.'

She looked up. 'Task?'

'You need a basket on your bicycle.' He took his dishes to the sink. 'Where did you leave it?'

'Against the gingerbread——' She stopped abruptly and her glance met his laughing eyes. They were now a light, clear blue, much nicer than the frowning ones.

'It *is* a bit over the top, isn't it?' He grinned. 'I call it the Tiverton folly.'

Caroline lowered her eyes. She concentrated on drinking his coffee; it was as delicious as she remembered.

After a quick glance at her downcast face, David rinsed his dishes. 'I'll see what I can find in the garage that might do.' He left the kitchen and Caroline remained sitting, sipping thoughtfully.

It really was none of her business, but it did seem a curious arrangement. If Henrietta Tiverton had David Hunter in her clutches why did she leave him alone to go off with other people? Who would ever want to leave David? Well, she *had* seemed rather odd. Perhaps he couldn't go with her. Doctors couldn't just rush off every which way at the drop of a hat. Maybe he just didn't want to go to Gloucestershire. This thought was strangely comforting, and she washed her own dishes in a more cheerful frame of mind. Leaving them to drain, she went out to see what he was going to do to the bicycle, carrying the music book with her. After all this effort, she wasn't going to lose it.

She found him with the bicycle across his lap, on the ground. He was trying to strap an old wicker basket to the handlebars without much success.

'Doesn't want to stay attached.' He was muttering to himself. The basket fell off and he retreated into the garage, returning with a box of metallic bolts and a heavy screwdriver.

Caroline watched as he resettled himself and sorted through the box. She perched herself on a small bench.

'David. . .' Her voice sounded small in her own ears.

He heard her use his name and his heart skipped a beat, but he kept his eyes on his work. He clearly remembered what had happened the last time she had spoken his name and he wouldn't repeat that mistake.

'Can I ask you a question?'

'Sure.' He kept his eyes on the troublesome basket.

'Do you think it's wrong of me to get music especially for one patient?'

'Wrong? Why should it be?' He looked up at her with a puzzled expression. He listened without interrupting to her account of the argument between Alison and Andrew and answered thoughtfully, 'I think I agree with Andrew.'

'But if I play Bach for Mr Vanijek, I'm doing the same thing.' She couldn't quite see the difference.

His answer came with a certainty. 'You've been playing for them all, and the Bach is for one patient but can be enjoyed by anyone else.' He thought for a moment. 'It's as if Alison bought a cake for all the children. She could choose little Ben's favourite kind of cake, to please him, but all the others could have a slice.'

'Oh. I hadn't thought of it that way.' She nodded. 'Sometimes people can love people, but it can be in a wrong way.'

He nodded silently and returned his attention to the problem of finding a bar to join two bolts. He spoke without looking up. 'Speaking of music—do you like opera?'

'Yes. Yes, I do,' Caroline answered readily.

'Would you like to go to *Freischütz*?' He kept his eyes on his hands.

'Oh. . . I don't know. . .when?' Caroline felt a little flustered.

'Next Thursday.'

'Oh. . .that's my day off.' It seemed a lovely idea, and after a long stretch on duty it would be good to get away from the hospital.

'Mmmm.' David maintained his concentration on his handling of the screwdriver. Braving Meg Clarke's teasing glance had been well worthwhile as he had attempted to make sense of the nurses' off-duty schedule. It had always looked like Eygptian hieroglyphics to him, and he had ignored Meg's chuckle as she had pointed out the relevant days with her finger tapping the symbols beside Caroline's name.

'Well. . .all right. Yes. I would like to go,' Caroline agreed. She did love opera, but hadn't been since Aunt Betty had become ill. She had a sudden idea. 'If we go on Thursday, I could visit my aunt and then meet you there.'

'Nonsense.' He looked up with a broad smile. 'We can drive up early and I'll go with you. I'd like to meet this Aunt Betty of yours.'

'All right.' Caroline felt pleased. She didn't look forward to another long train journey, and she would like her aunt to meet David Hunter. She happily hugged the music book to her chest. She couldn't remember the opera. She thought it had a popular overture. 'What's the story?'

'The what? Oh, you mean the Weber. It's a sort of down-market Wagner. Lots of Bavarian drinking songs.' He gave the basket a firm tug and stood up, lifting the bicycle upright.

As he stood up he suddenly startled Caroline and a flock of birds in a nearby tree by bursting into a strong, lilting melody. She laughed with delight.

He stopped singing and glinted down at her. 'That's my song—the hunters' chorus. Good tub-thumping stuff.'

'Yes, I recognise it.' Caroline, still laughing lightly,

stood up to admire the basket, now firmly bolted into place. 'I just hope you don't intend to join in with the performance!'

'I will attempt to control myself, as difficult as that may be.' He smiled with mock humility and gave the bicycle a quick rattle. 'This should do it.'

'Yes, it's perfect. Thank you.' Caroline put the book into the basket. 'I should be getting back. I have to be in by two, to change for work.'

'You look quite beautiful as you are.' His comment caused a deep flush to deepen her cheeks and she concentrated on steering the bicycle to the front of the house. 'Do you know the way?'

'Yes, I remember.' Hoping her face had not become even redder, Caroline hurriedly mounted and started to pedal away, with a brief wave. How well she remembered every inch of the way back to Castleview! It seemed just as beautiful today, and she flew back through the fields with the freshening wind flowing straight through her singing heart.

CHAPTER EIGHT

NOTHING could dampen Caroline's sunny spirits during the following few days. Finding on Monday afternoon that Osbert looked cleaned and polished merely added an extra glow to her quiet happiness. It seemed that a local piano turner had arrived on Monday morning and Meg had been relieved to show him off the ward at noon—'We may not be the quietest ward in Castleview, but hours of repeated plonking we *don't* need!'

Caroline was delighted with Osbert's new voice. He had a lovely deepness in the lower register and she eagerly started on her Bach practice after the evening drinks had been given out on Monday evening. As she had hoped, Anton Vanijek came in to listen and smiled at her enthusiasm. He said nothing but stayed for half an hour before leaving, thanking her with his unwavering politeness.

Even Martin seemed more outgoing. David had written a note in his file about the progress of their daily interviews. Apparently the boy's disturbed behaviour had occurred as a reaction to a break-up with his girlfriend. Caroline knew it was important that she maintain the regular periods of time she sat with him so he would learn that not everyone rejected him.

She had begun to give up hope that the boy would ever speak to her again, when she heard his voice over her shoulder. She had been flipping through a music book, marking some tempo changes while she sat beside him in the day-room.

'What are all those squiggly things, then?'

She looked up. His voice was not as harsh as she remembered. 'Which things do you mean, Martin?'

'Them.' He pointed to the notes on the stave.

'Those are musical sounds—at least, they are a way of writing down certain sounds.'

'You mean you can tell what the sound is, by looking at them blobs?' He sounded surprised and Caroline smiled.

'Yes, in a way. Would you like me to show you?' She was not going to let such an opportunity slip by.

'OK.' He followed her into the music-room, as the staff and patients had come to call the old workroom. Caroline played a few notes and demonstrated the equivalent notes on the book, but Martin quickly lost interest. He turned away, to look at Terry's small set of drums.

'I like *them*.' As he spoke, Caroline followed his gaze and nodded.

'Terry could show you how to make good sounds from the drums. All I can do is thump and bang a bit. I'll ask him to show you when he comes in.'

The following evening, Terry accepted Martin's interested observation and allowed him to tap out a light rhythm during yet another rendition of 'Tipperary'. The harmony of the enlarging group of men singing each evening was beginning to improve. Caroline was wondering if the addition of female voices might help, when her thoughts were spoken aloud by Bob.

'Nurse. . .' He approached her during a break in their

habitual singing of music hall favourites. She had been delighted to see him join the group and he seemed to enjoy adding a light baritone to the lower descants. He also seemed less fidgety when he was singing, although as soon as the music stopped his fine jerking movements would begin again. 'I was thinking. . .do you think. . .?'

Caroline smiled encouragingly and he burst out in a rush of words, 'Could we have ladies in our group? They'd add more life. . .like. . .' He subsided as a few of the men laughed at his words.

'I quite agree, Bob.' Caroline spoke quickly through a few ribald remarks she could hear in the background. 'How do you think we could arrange to have some ladies?'

'We could ask over at Whitney.' Bob's face seemed to colour slightly and Caroline could hear a few more quiet remarks from the others, but they sounded teasing. She was aware that the patients had a network of knowledge about each other that staff did not always share.

'I think that is a splendid idea. I'll ask Sister and perhaps you could enquire at Whitney. Is there anyone you could ask?' She suspected there might be a specific reason for Bob's suggestion, judging from the chatter of his fellow patients. She was delighted to think that this nervous man had a woman friend.

The strange but extremely pleasant feeling of light-headedness she was feeling continued until the Thursday. She had the morning to herself to prepare for David's arrival in the early afternoon. She sang happily to herself as she sorted through her limited wardrobe.

Caroline was secretly glad of the privacy in the quiet residence. For some reason she was not eager to talk about David Hunter with anyone else.

The morning was spent in the luxury of an hour's bath. One of the few good things about late shifts was having the bathroom to yourself for as long as you wanted. She splurged on some of Alison's richly lathered bubble bath and played happily with the blanket of airy foam. She knew she was behaving like a child but decided she didn't care. She felt like the night before

Christmas—filled to the brim with anticipation of magical gifts to come.

As she bounded out of the bath and ran lightly down the corridor back to her room she thought she heard the tread of a man's footsteps going down the stairs at the rear of the building.

'Andrew?' she called, hopefully. She would like to talk with Andrew; she hadn't seen him since his argument with Alison. There was no answer and she shrugged before going into her room and automatically sliding the door bolt across. She didn't want to be interrupted as she planned her appearance very carefully.

Critical appraisal of the results of her planning resulted in a satisfied nod. She had plaited her hair high on her head and allowed the thick braid to fall down her back. The tiny pearl earrings picked up the glowing flower-buds on the embroidered sleeveless waistcoat which looked very rich against the white long-sleeved blouse. A bracelet of fine seed-pearls on her wrist under the lacy cuff made her feel very delicate and feminine.

Caroline looked at her mirrored image with a guilty grin. You are behaving like an adolescent, she told her shining face. As if this were your very first date and it's all a romantic dream. She shook her head firmly and picked up her jacket. That certainly puts practicality back into the ensemble, she thought, as she left to wait downstairs for David.

She didn't have long to wait. He arrived at the door with his usual burst of energy, and as she moved out of the lounge towards him she was smiling broadly but stopped, flustered, at the sudden warmth of his gaze.

'You are indeed a beauty, Caro.' His voice was husky and he looked at her for what seemed very long minutes. She flushed under his look but couldn't move past as his large frame was blocking the door.

His hand moved to lightly touch her ear. 'A perfect pearl of a girl.'

She tingled slightly at his touch and felt her face was probably beginning to resemble the colour of her waistcoat.

His tone lightened. 'Your chariot awaits.' Caroline

allowed him to tuck her hand under his elbow as they left the building. She stopped and laughed out loud at the car parked at bottom of the steps. It was a clean and sparkling small orange tin box.

'Her name is St Christina.' He carefully guided her into the tiny passenger seat.

'All right, why Christina?' His joking repartee was a relief from the intensity of his response to her appearance.

'The patron saint of travellers—female variety.' He wedged himself carefully into the driver's seat beside her. 'Only a woman could be as faithful as this put-upon automobile.'

Caroline was acutely aware of his closeness in the small car. She could smell the freshness of a slightly pine-scented aftershave and the warmth of his sleeve brushed her shoulder. She felt she was practically sitting on his lap and carefully moved her knee to avoid being bumped by his large hand on the gear stick.

As the small car bounced through the gates, they both looked over at the porter's lodge.

'No sign of Charlie again. I suppose it's too much to hope he's doing the pharmacy round.' His statement sounded cheerful and Caroline relaxed. He sounded as light-hearted as she felt.

'I don't think he's been seen for days. The afternoon staff are picking up the box before they come on duty, at least on Folkestone.' As she answered, it occurred to her that conversation might be a bit difficult with this man as the only thing they had in common was their work. She mentioned Bob's suggestion for enlargement of their singing group and smiled at David's response.

'Nothing more natural. Get all the women you can. My Welsh grandfather would turn in his grave to hear me say it, but I prefer a mixed chorus any time.' They were heading out to the main highway and chatted easily about various patients until he asked her for directions to the nursing home as they drove through the city.

As they walked past the receptionist in the central lobby of the nursing home, Caroline noticed the clean hand-embroidered tablecloth on the round table in the

hall, under the massive bouquet of yellow chrysanthe-
mums and the various potted plants along the deep
window-sills.

They passed along the corridor and headed down
towards the end room where Aunt Betty was staying,
sharing with one other patient. They passed a room
where the cheerful chirping of a pet canary could be
heard and David raised a quizzical eyebrow as he caught
Caroline's glance.

She suspected he was probably considering the possibility of having birds on his admission wards at
Castleview. His eyes had been glancing around with
deceptive casualness and she knew the unit was being
examined professionally. He never stops looking for
ideas to adopt, she thought. She was beginning to
understand how his mind worked, beneath the calm,
friendly exterior. No matter how relaxed he might
appear, that brain of his never stopped ticking.

Entering the end room, Caroline walked quickly to
the side of a bed where a frail old lady lay motionless
with her hands outside a tidily tucked-in blanket. David
remained at the foot of the bed, watching the grey,
deeply lined face on the pillow very carefully. He noted
how the eyes opened as Caroline greeted her aunt,
allowing a brief glimpse of watery, pale brown eyes
before the blue-veined lids closed and the face regained
the image of a waxen effigy.

He silently moved to the opposite side of the bed,
pulled a chair close and sat down, reaching for the old
lady's hand. As she saw him sit, Caroline smiled across
at him and introduced him to her aunt.

'This is David Hunter, Aunt Betty. He's come to see
you, as well.' She talked as easily as she always had to
her aunt. It was simple to pretend that she could hear
and sometimes Caroline even imagined various answers.
She rarely felt the conversation was one-sided and, even
though anyone listening might feel she was chattering
absolute nonsense, Caroline always found her mono-
logues strangely reassuring and comforting. Even talking
into an abyss of silence could be therapeutic, she supposed—so much for the theory of needing an active
listener.

Still, she was glad of David's presence across the bed. He had clasped Aunt Betty's limp hand and settled himself down comfortably beside the bed. He had kept hold of the frail hand and Caroline thought how compassionate this particular young doctor was.

In this instance, she had misinterpreted David Hunter's primary motive for holding on to the old lady's hand. He had slipped his fingers unobtrusively up under her thin wrist and kept a light, even pressure on a clearly felt pulse. The knotted veins showed a visible pulse, but he preferred to keep his eyes on Aunt Betty's face as Caroline talked. The information he received through his fingers was somewhat different from that through his visual observation.

Caroline continued to talk to her aunt, telling her of various happenings at the hospital including short funny stories of her friends. She had never discussed any deeply disturbing events, partly because of the continuous audience of the elderly woman in next bed beside the wall. Caroline always remembered that the last sense to be detected in an unconscious patient was that of hearing, and she could never be certain that the apparently confused, deaf old woman just a few feet away was as inert as she appeared to be. After all, it was this belief and hope that kept bringing her back to Aunt Betty's side to tell her stories just as she would have done had they still been at home.

After about half an hour, Caroline sighed and started to tell her aunt that it was time for them to leave. There had been no visible change in the pale face turned towards Caroline on the pillow, but David Hunter suddenly stood up and firmly but softly said. 'Goodbye, Aunt Betty.' To Caroline's surprise there was a visible flutter of the closed eyelids.

'Oh, David! She heard you! Aunt Betty heard you!' Caroline was delighted. She had always hoped that her stories had been heard, but she could never be sure. It must have been the suddenness with which he had arisen that had provoked a startled response.

'Yes, indeed.' Keeping his voice low, firm and speaking clearly, David kept his eyes on the still unmoving

face. 'It was a pleasure to meet you, Mrs Denmer. I am
sure we will meet again.' He grasped the slight hand
warmly, then tucked it carefully under the blanket.

Caroline watched as the tall young man treated her
aunt like a china doll, and she was grateful for his
gentleness. She had a sudden vision of him tucking in
his own child to sleep securely, and she felt a sharp surge
of longing that she quickly suppressed.

As they left the room, Caroline smiled broadly at
David, grateful for his companionship. She had never
brought anyone with her to visit Aunt Betty; this would
be the first time she had brought a 'young man' to her
aunt for many years. It was a pity that Aunt Betty could
not give her usually astute opinions of the suitability of
any of her 'dates'. Caroline giggled softly to herself.

'And what do you find so funny?' David's voice was
warm in her ear as he casually reached around her
shoulders to open the swing doors for them to leave.

She glanced up and was surprised at the grave,
thoughtful expression on his face. 'I was remembering
her reaction when I brought home my friends from
school.' Caroline was walking slowly back to the car.
'She usually had some very observant remarks to make,
and I was wondering what she would have made of you.'

'Hmm. I wonder. . .' His voice was non-committal
and he moved smoothly into place behind the small
driving-wheel. As he started up the motor, he turned his
head towards Caroline. 'I have a telephone call I need to
make before we go on. Do you mind if we stop for a
bit?'

'Of course not.' Caroline was surprised, as surely he
could have made his call from the home, while she sat
with her aunt, but since he was driving it was up to him
how soon they started.

'Good, that's done. Now, how about food?' David
returned quickly and again lowered himself carefully
into the small car.

Caroline grinned at his discomfort. This man should
have a long, large car in which to breathe, not the
minuscule automobile they were driving in.

'And what's so funny this time, may I ask?' They were heading back to the West End.

'I was thinking you need more space—a bigger car.'

'Tell that to my bank manager.' He slowly took his place behind a large lorry that threatened to bury them in black exhaust fumes. 'Enough of this.' David swerved the small car with expert skill and whipped around the large vehicle, slipping in behind a green Porsche. 'That's better. Almost as good as the bike, this.'

She looked over at David. 'Where are we going?'

'There's a good pizza place near the opera and we can hole up there until curtain time. OK?' He kept his eyes on the road.

'Fine.' Caroline had decided to agree to whatever he suggested, and found that her trust had not been misplaced. The 'pizza place' turned out to be an elegant Italian restaurant with attractive soft brownwood panelling on the walls and cheerful green and red striped tablecloths.

She noticed the napkins were the same shade as her waistcoat, as David helped her off with her jacket. It seemed he recognised this fact as well.

'Again, perfect. . .' His eyes were once more looking at her with that intense look, and to hide her embarrassment she stared down at the menu.

Caroline willingly allowed David to order, which she was astonished to hear him do in Italian. A short but vociferous conversation with the waiter followed, and Caroline watched in uncomprehending silence.

'Just making friends.' He smiled at her. 'I asked for extra cheese and tomato on yours. There was a slight discussion about the type of cheese required.'

'I didn't know you spoke Italian.' Caroline could hear herself sounding trite. In the soft amber glow of the nearly empty restaurant the need to make conversation suddenly seemed very important. She found herself oddly tongue-tied as she looked at the clean lines of the face across the table.

He gave a small shrug of his shoulders. 'German would be more useful, but I haven't managed to get very far with it.'

Wondering if there were any mountains in Germany, Caroline maintained an expression of polite interest.

'Understanding the analytical boys needs German.' He was talking partly to himself and Caroline picked up a topic she wanted to know about.

'Analytical boys? You mean psychoanalysis?'

He nodded. 'Can't get very far without some knowledge of German in that field. And that's where the money is.' He sighed lightly.

'Money?' Thinking she sounded like an echoing parrot, Caroline repeated his word. Was he talking about private practice? She had a sudden hope that he wasn't. 'I don't really understand much about psychoanalysis.'

'Easy, really. Ah. . .' Two very large pizzas had been placed in front of them. Caroline gulped. There really was a very great deal to eat. 'What would you like to know?' He was picking up his knife and fork and looked up at her.

'Well, I've read about the Freudian view of the unconscious mind, but it didn't make a great deal of sense.' Caroline wondered where to make a start on the circle of food in front of her.

'Ach, so. Herr Professor will explain.' David waved his knife as if at a blackboard and pointed down at the pizza. 'This is a complete circle. So let it represent a person, all complete, everything in place. Lots of cheese, tomato, mushrooms, anchovies, pepperoni, even some onions from what I can see.' He peered a little closer at the pizza. 'And some capers as well.' He looked up, smiling. 'A very well-rounded person indeed.'

Caroline watched him, fascinated. He was entertaining her, she knew, but she did want to understand.

'Now, according to Freud we have three major sections to our mind—the id, which is mainly pepperoni with lots of spice,' he moved bits of sausage to the left of his pizza, 'and the superego which is full of, let's say, anchovies.' A large pile of anchovies ended up on the right-hand side of the pizza.

'And the ego is the bit in between—stands between the pepperoni and the anchovies. That's the referee or umpire, if you like.

'The spicy pepperoni in the id loves fun and mis-chief—that's the child in all of us.' He moved his knife over to the right-hand side. 'And the nasty-looking anchovies don't really approve of all that fun. They are the rules and regulations we've learned over the years.'

'When we're growing up, you mean?'

'Yes. When we're born, we're just a bundle of pure id, all pepperoni. We want what we want when we want it. No anchovies at all—they get added later.' He grinned at Caroline. 'A pizza with only pepperoni would be tastier than one with just anchovies, but they really taste much better mixed.'

'Do you mean that the superego tells us what is right and wrong?'

'Precisely. But sometimes there are too many anchov-ies and not enough pepperoni. The mix must be just right, to be healthy, or the best eating.' He removed some of the anchovies to the middle. 'And if you don't mind, I think I will start to demolish this pizza-person, before he goes cold on me.'

'How can some people have too many anchovies?' Caroline giggled as she watched him redistribute the ingredients. Her cheese and tomato pizza-person was very good.

'They are too strict on themselves. They don't have much fun because the anchovies are stronger than the pepperoni and won't let the spice of life come to the fore, if you'll pardon the phrase.' He had started on a rapid decimation of the lecture material.

'Like our violinist?' Caroline knew better than to mention a patient's name in a public place, but she couldn't let this chance of understanding pass.

'Yes, I think so. Whereas our drummer friend is mainly pepperoni. He doesn't like anchovies much.'

'And the umpire?'

'Perhaps I should have said cook. That's us. Some-times we replace a weak umpire or strengthen him.' He chewed for a moment. 'The cook redistributes the ingredients, so that one half doesn't overpower the other.'

'That sounds like music. A conductor does the same

thing, so the sound is right—not too brassy or shrill.'
Caroline used a field she could understand, as the pizzas
were rapidly disappearing.

'Good. I agree. And maybe our music can work that
way. If the anchovy person can rediscover his pepperoni
sense of delight and our pepperoni person can accept
some anchovy discipline, we might have achieved a much
better mix of ingredients.' He patted himself contentedly. 'Now for the sweet—pure id, if you like.'

'Not for me.' Caroline didn't have room for any more
food. She was thinking of what he had said. Aunt Betty's
proverbs had always had a strong sense of right and
wrong. 'Is it wrong to be sure of what you think is right?'

'Not necessarily. What are you thinking of?'

'My aunt. She always knew what she thought was
right.'

'Tell me more about Aunt Betty.' He made a brief
motion to a waiter and coffee arrived on their table.
Caroline was delighted it was *cappuccino*. Probably an id
drink, with all that sweet cream, she thought.

'Well, she brought me up. I think I said that. She was
like a mother to me. My parents died when I was born
so she adopted me.' Caroline blew at the creamy froth
and watched the bits of chocolate dance in white bubbles.

'Was there an uncle? I notice she is Mrs Denmer.' He
had seen the name on the bed and was watching Caroline
carefully.

'Yes. . .' Caroline paused. 'I don't remember much
about him. He lived upstairs. He had a back injury of
some sort and was in a wheelchair. I don't know what it
was. He died when I was about six.' Caroline looked
down at her coffee and frowned.

'You didn't like him?' David's voice was casual.

'No. No, I didn't. But I don't know why, really.' She
never could account for her dislike of that rarely seen
figure in the house. 'I didn't see him much and then, of
course, he died. So I pretty well forgot all about him.'
She looked up. 'That's all there is to tell. There isn't
much. A very ordinary life—school, nursing training
and now I'm here.'

'So you are.' His warm smile reached into her heart and she smiled happily back at him.

'Now it's your turn. Tell me about your Welsh grandfather—the one who wouldn't like women in our singing group.'

David laughed lightly. 'I never knew him. Apparently he could sing and my mother says I took after him. My boy soprano voice got me into a choir school which opened a few doors, so I'm grateful to him.' He took a slow sip of his coffee and regarded her quietly before continuing, 'I mentioned that my father was an alcoholic.'

Caroline nodded. She still didn't know how to respond to this statement, so she remained silent.

'He died, eventually, of cirrhosis.' David paused and looked into his coffee-cup for a moment before continuing in an even voice, 'He had a habit of beating up my mother and I swore that when I grew up I would knock the stuffing out of him.' He smiled wryly. 'He died before I got big enough.'

'Oh, David, I'm so sorry.' Impulsively, Caroline touched his hand. She had a vision of a very small boy seething with rage.

He nodded. 'I think why I am telling you this, Caro, is to say something. . .' Again he paused. 'I respond very strongly. . .whenever I see a woman, or anyone else really, being attacked.' He looked across the table at her and covered her hand with his on the table. 'I had forgotten that old feeling, but it came back. When you were in the kitchen. . .'

Caroline looked at him solemnly. She knew that what he was telling her was very important. He was giving something private of himself and she felt her heart go out to him. She longed to be able to give him something of equal value in return, but there was nothing she could think of, other than her compassion.

'I just wanted you to know.' His smile lightened as he looked over at her serious face. 'I'm no shining knight, but I do tend to leap to the defence—sometimes without considering the consequences, or how other people concerned might feel about it.'

Caroline nodded. She remembered his watchfulness
when Martin had arrived on the ward. She thought he
was indeed a shining knight but, if he didn't want to
think so, she could always keep her belief to herself.

'I'm. . . I'm grateful. . .' How could she express her
feelings? He was the finest man she had ever met, but
she had no words to tell him what she was feeling. She
could merely look at him silently.

'I think it's time to retreat to the world of fantasy.' He
grinned at her and Caroline blinked, at a loss. When she
saw him motion for the bill, she smiled. He meant the
opera. She was beginning to retreat too far into her own
quite lovely and unreal dream world.

As they walked arm in arm around the corner to join
the crowds beginning to gather for the evening performance, Caroline felt that she was almost walking on air.
With her arm tucked under the warmth and solidity of
his, she felt very tiny and precious. It was a foolish
feeling, she knew, but quite delicious. She skipped
lightly and laughed quietly.

'Dancing in the streets, then?' He looked down at the
shining eyes of this golden girl.

'I feel like it!' She really did feel as if she could float
away in a rainbow-coloured bubble. Everything about
the evening was glowing with an incandescent halo and
the appearance of the brightly lit open doors of the opera
house only reinforced her impression of a fairyland. She
was in a world of beautiful people in sumptuous dresses
surrounded by great music. Heaven couldn't be so very
different from what she saw around her.

David guided her through the crowds and they found
their seats in the upper circle. Caroline was delighted
and David silently congratulated himself. Those shining
brown eyes were well worth his recently acquired bank
overdraft.

As they waited for the orchestra to settle, Caroline sat
on the edge of her seat. David watched her with pleasure.
She seemed so delighted with the anticipation; he prayed
she would not be disappointed.

His worry was unfounded. Caroline was enchanted
with the performance. The overture was everything she

remembered and the soaring themes were played with restrained power. As she heard the opening shouts of the peasants' chorus, she realised that they were to be included in one of the rare moments—a performance that reached above the norm.

She entered whole-heartedly into the legend being unfolded before them—the danger in the wolf's glen, the heroine's fear for the hero, the evil devil bargaining for a man's soul. She found the heroine's prayer very moving and the ending thoroughly satisfying.

The applause of the audience was unrestrained and the singers acknowledged the verdict with suitable grace.

'They know they put in a good one, they must know it!' Caroline turned to David as she was clapping enthusiastically.

He smiled and nodded; he had been hoping for this, as he had deliberately chosen the final performance and suspected the performers might produce that something extra special. He knew Caroline would recognise the spark of such music and he sighed with relief. Her pleasure gave him a deep happienss. She was laughing with a freedom he knew she had, but had never seen. He had hoped music would be the key and he seemed to have guessed rightly.

They followed the departing crowd and walked through the streets to the Mini. Caroline settled happily in the now familiar tiny car and hummed the heroine's prayer melody. She would like to find the music for that one.

As they headed out into the dark countryside from the lights of the city, David began to override her humming with a stronger version of the hunters' chorus. Caroline laughed and let him win that particular battle.

He then switched to the duet and Caroline attempted to remember the heroine's part. She couldn't match his control of the melody with her light voice, but they managed a reasonable rendition by the time they were nearing the hospital.

David then started the hermit's melody and Caroline tried to correct him. Surely that high note was wrong.

He was just showing off. She sang the lower key and he laughed. 'Wrong! It goes da de deeeee, not da de dum.'

'It doesn't!'

'Does!'

'Doesn't!'

'Prove it!'

'I can't prove it. I just know.'

'You don't know, woman. *I* know. . .' He swerved the car off to a country road. '*I'll* prove it.'

Caroline watched as they turned away from the hospital. So they were going to the farmhouse. She couldn't object; she didn't really want this evening to end. She would be happy to drive forever in the small car filled with music.

'I'll prove it, you'll see.' He stopped the car and led the way through the kitchen door. 'You go upstairs and get the recording.' She glared at him. 'Yes, of course I have a recording, so I *know* you are wrong.' He waved her out of the kitchen. 'Go, woman. See for yourself.'

Caroline ran up the stairs to the back corridor. She reached the small study and headed for the LPs. True enough, he had the full rendition. She looked through to find the right place.

By the time he came up, bearing a tray of hastily made sandwiches and tea, she had started the record and was curled up on the floor, listening intently. 'It brings it all back. They *were* good tonight, weren't they?'

'Hmm. We were lucky.' He sat down beside her. 'Just wait, you'll see.' They munched and listened in silence. Caroline leaned back against the wall and closed her eyes. She could picture everything they had seen and it was as good as being there again.

David watched her silently. So she's back in your sanctuary, this little sparrow. He sighed silently to himself. He would willingly allow the world to stop for the rest of his life and stay just as it was at this very moment.

Caroline opened her eyes suddenly. He was right! The disputed melody came serenely out of the speakers and she glanced over at him. He was stretched out on the floor with his eyes closed and a wide grin of triumph on his face.

She gave a short snort of defeat and reached to heave a pillow at that self-satisfied smirk. As her arm was raised to fling the soft pillow, she felt her elbow grasped firmly and she ended up clasped against his chest.

'Oh, no, you don't!' His eyes were twinkling. 'I expect at least the semblance of gracious defeat. Now, admit you were wrong. . .'

Caroline felt her arms tingle in the warmth of his grasp and she leaned slightly backwards, feeling flustered. Did he expect her to arm wrestle with him? She laughed to cover her confusion. 'All right, you win. I was wrong.'

'Good girl. Now. . .what do I win?' His grin was teasing. His hands had slid down her arms and were imprisoning her hands.

'I. . . I didn't know there was a p. . .prize.' Caroline felt her breathing oddly constricted by a sudden jolt of her heart. His nearness seemed to make her senses whirl and she resisted an impulse to bury her head against that familiar shoulder and have his arms enclose her again.

With his clear eyes fastened on her face, David gently raised her hands to his lips. 'No prize, Caro. Just my satisfaction.' He sat up quickly and held her lightly by the shoulders. Before she could think what was happening, she felt the touch of his lips on her forehead. 'Winning is always a satisfaction, especially when it's a certainty.' He grinned at her and reached over to the tray. 'Now eat—it's been a long time since the pizza.'

She stayed seated on the floor and reached for another sandwich. As David went over to the stereo to remove the record, she watched his free and easy movements. Her forehead was still warm from his touch and she deliberately controlled a desire to put her fingers on the spot he had kissed.

He was the most beautiful man she had ever met and he seemed to be able to see right through her. And I want him to, she thought. I really want him to. . . She pushed away such thoughts. He was just charming and friendly and kind and fun and. . .and probably just flirting.

Caroline swallowed a bite of her sandwich slowly. Over-reacting more than a bit, girl. Cool down. Just as she was beginning to wonder if her hormone levels were developing a strange disorder, she heard the quiet ringing of a telephone in the next room.

As David left to answer it, Caroline moved over to the couch. Through the door she could hear him answering in monosyllables. This evening could be shorter than she wanted; the conversation sounded professional. Wanted? She didn't know what she wanted. Except. . .

'Sorry, Caro. Duty calls.' David reappeared and quickly turned off the stereo.

'A patient?' She quickly reached for her coat. Never fall for a doctor, she thought. Sick people always have first claim.

At his nod, she added, 'Folkestone?'

'No. In London.' His reply was abrupt and Caroline felt a slight twinge of irritation.

'Oh. A private patient.' So he would drive all that way back to see a rich person waving a fat cheque.

'You could say that.' He sounded distant and pre-occupied and Caroline followed him down to the Mini. The evening seemed to have lost its glow and she sat silently beside him during the drive back to the hospital.

As he slowly stopped in front of the residence, she turned to him. This time she would not run in, flustered with embarrassment. 'It was a perfect day, David.' She looked at his angular face outlined in the reflection of the porch light and her voice softened. 'Thank you.'

His smile was tender as he picked up her hand, holding it lightly in his warm clasp. 'My honour, Caro, and my deepest pleasure.'

As his lips brushed her fingertips, she felt her hand tremble, and she reached up to touch that fly-away lock of fair hair that always fell over his ear. 'David. . .?' She breathed his name through parted lips.

'Yes, Caro?' His mouth softly caressed the palm of her hand. He looked up at her face, hearing the appeal in her voice.

'Will you. . .p-please kiss me?' Her voice sounded very tiny and small.

His answer was to breathe her name softly as his mouth moved to graze her earlobes. She felt a warm brush on her brow before his lips slowly descended to meet hers. His kiss was slow and warm and she felt a delicious sensation spread through her limbs as he moved his mouth over hers, caressing its softness.

She responded to the pressure of his lips with eagerness to welcome the tenderness of his softly exploring movements. She felt an overwhelming desire to be part of him, and twined her fingers in his silky hair to hold him closer.

As his hand gently cupped the warm curve under the velvet she felt her breast surge under his gentle massage.

'Oh, David. . .' She breathed against his neck as his mouth searched for and found the beating pulse in the hollow of her throat.

'My love. . .my love.' His voice was husky and he raised his head to look deeply into her dark eyes, lashes glistening in the dim light. He tilted her head back against his arm and drew her closer. His mouth covered hers hungrily, and as his lips parted hers she felt an aching need deep within her as she reached up to hold him tightly. She pressed her swelling breasts against his chest and felt his strong hands slide around her waist to hold her against his hardness. As she reached up to wind her arms around his neck, Caroline felt a tiny spasm at the base of her spine. No, she moaned silently. No. No, I won't let it. I won't.

She clung tightly as he raised his head slowly. 'Caro? What is it, my love?' He had felt her shudder like this before.

'N. . .nothing. It's nothing.' She choked the words against his shoulder. 'Please don't let me go. Please hold me.'

'I won't let you go, Caro. Never.' David kept a hand lightly over her heart without moving. 'Tell me. Tell me what you are feeling.' His words were whispered against the smooth cheek buried in his neck.

'It's just my. . .flutters.' Her words were muffled and he bent to brush his lips against her cheek.

He tasted the saltiness of her tears. 'Your flutters. . .'

He raised his large hand to touch her face. 'These are bad feelings?'

She nodded mutely and he brushed the corners of her eyes with a soft stroke of his thumb. 'Do they get worse?' He smiled gently at the semi-hidden face.

'Yes. . .' Caroline sighed. She had never told anyone before, but she couldn't bear to hurt this wonderful man. He needed to know. He had a right to know. 'I want. . .' She stopped.

'I know, Caro.' His voice was soft and soothing.

'But I can't.' She could feel her tears starting again. 'The flutters. . .' She swallowed. How could she explain what she didn't understand herself?

'So.' David leaned back slightly, watching her with a calm smile. 'So. . .do you know when these feelings start?'

Caroline shook her head. 'Not always. They just come.' She tried to smile at him but she couldn't meet his eyes. 'It's just me. Stupid me.' She moved away from him. 'I try to ignore them, but that never works. I thought. . .'

David brushed a strand of hair from her forehead. 'Ignoring feelings is never a good idea. Understanding them is our business, isn't it?'

She attempted to smile and glanced up at his face. He was looking at her with such tenderness that her heart ached.

'We will try an experiment.' With a smile, he quietly kissed the tip of her nose. 'Any bad flutters?'

Caroline shook her head and smiled more freely.

'Good. So we will be content, my love.' He folded his arms around her comfortably. 'We will be patient. In any case, I'm afraid we have no choice.' His lips brushed her forehead as he spoke. 'I'll have a heavy workload for the next few weeks and we won't have a chance for a while to carry through with our. . .understanding of your. . .flutters.'

He looked down at her with a dark intensity in his eyes that warmed her heart. 'You will be in my thoughts every waking moment, my love, and probably most of the sleeping ones as well.' As he kissed her lips softly,

Caroline felt his tenderness enclose her like a soft, familiar blanket.

'And now, goodnight, my little sparrow. It has indeed been a beautiful and quite perfect day.' He gently released her and got out of the car.

As he opened the door for her, she suddenly remembered. 'I've never said thank you for the bicycle.'

David gave a deep chuckle. 'I consider myself thanked, Caro. Sleep well.' His lips brushed her mouth with the lightest whisper of a kiss and he turned to drive away in the small bouncing car.

Caroline, watching him leave, thought that the Mini looked just as she felt—full of life and energy. Carry him safely, she whispered into the darkness as she turned to go in.

Opening the door, she was astonished to see all the corridor lights on and she could hear voices coming from the lounge. As she stood uncertainly inside the door, the figure of the senior tutor appeared.

'Oh, Caroline, good. We have been waiting for you. Could you come in here, please?'

Her voice sounded sombre and businesslike. Caroline followed Jean Mansin into the lounge with a sudden twinge of anxiety. What could be happening?

CHAPTER NINE

THERE was an uneasy silence in the lounge as Caroline looked around at the solemn faces of her classmates. As far as she could see, most of the group were present; Annabelle and Tracey were seated together, with Tracey still in her party dress, which meant she must have also just returned from an evening out.

Caroline hugged her jacket around her and looked past the girls. Andrew was hunched on the edge of the settee and Caroline hurriedly went over to sit in the empty space beside him. She noticed Barbara and Tom seated behind, both looking pale and strained. Beth, across from them, looked confused and very sleepy.

'What's happened?' Caroline whispered to Andrew.

'Alison's gone.' His reply was muttered in a very low voice, nevertheless the acute ears of the tutor heard him.

'Yes, Caroline. Alison has left and I was hoping you might have some idea where she might have gone.'

'Left?' Caroline was confused. 'I didn't know. . .'

Jean Mansin's eyes watched her carefully before she nodded. 'I did not think that you did. But I was hoping she might have said something, to any one of you.' She looked around the group of silent students.

Annabelle shuffled her slippered feet; Caroline realised she must have been asleep after her long shift. 'She wasn't saying very much to any one of us.' Annabelle glanced over at Beth who shook her head slowly. 'Maybe Andrew—she liked you. . .' Her voice trailed off as she glanced at Andrew's downcast face.

'Yes.' He gave a deep sigh and looked up at Jean Mansin. 'I didn't know what she was planning, if it was planned.'

The tutor acknowledged his comment with a brief inclination of her head. 'We won't know that until we find her, and we must find her. Do any of you know, or can you think of, a place she would go?'

Caroline was perplexed. If Alison had left unexpectedly there must be a good reason. She couldn't understand why everyone should be so shocked. Students must have left before this, perhaps as suddenly.

While the other students talked among themselves, Caroline turned to Andrew. 'Why the midnight meeting? It can't be all that strange, surely?'

Andrew looked at her with a serious expression. 'She took Ben.'

'Took Ben? Who do you mean? The patient she told us about?'

Andrew nodded. Caroline was struck silent. She had realised Alison had been fond of the child, but this was kidnapping! She looked at Andrew in horror. What could Alison have done with Ben?

He was looking at Miss Mansin. 'As far as I know, her

family has several homes.' He paused and added quietly, 'I think there's one in Switzerland.'

Jean Mansin sighed. 'Thank you, Andrew. We have tried to contact her family, but haven't been successful yet. We will have to follow it through.' She looked around at them all. 'I apologise for gathering you together so urgently. I think we have done everything we can for the time being. I will let you know what is happening, as soon as I have any further information.'

She slowly rose from her chair and left them to discuss Alison among themselves. Caroline had a brief moment of sympathy for the tutor. The implications of Alison's behaviour could be far reaching, especially if she had taken the patient out of the country.

'Do you think she would, Andrew—take him to Switzerland?' she asked anxiously.

'Who knows?' He shrugged sadly. 'She's a law unto herself.' He looked at her with a wry smile. 'I wonder if it was anything I said, or if I could have handled that discussion better. I suppose I'll never know, really.'

'Did you tell Miss Mansin about that?' Caroline had not thought of their argument while the tutor was present.

'Yes.' He nodded and looked down at his hands with a glum expression. 'It never occurred to me that she would go so far.'

'Why now? What made her want to take him away now?'

'His father came to collect him.' Andrew smiled at Caroline briefly. 'In spite of what Alison told us, the family seems to be very caring and they wanted him home with the others. The mother was home on leave from her treatment and missed her youngest. It had all been arranged and when they came to pick him up, he was gone. So was Alison, but it took a bit of time to put one and one together.'

They sat silently thinking and Caroline felt a heavy cloak of sadness slowly drift over her shoulders. Wherever Alison was, Caroline could only hope that the child was safe. Poor Alison—she seemed to love Ben but it had led her to such a desperately unhappy action.

★ ★ ★

Although she saw David regularly on the ward, Caroline did not have an opportunity to talk with him alone. She knew he would have heard about Alison; Castleview had the same effective gossip and communication channels as any large institution. She would have liked to have heard his opinion. He might be able to explain such behaviour, but he always seemed to be rushing from one meeting to another. He would wave and smile, but not stop, the long strides taking him to the next crisis that needed a decision.

Caroline found that her own workload kept her happy enough. Her case study on Martin was proceeding evenly. He seemed more relaxed with her and she was recording each short conversation they had during their time after tea. They talked only of light, inconsequential things, but Caroline knew that the fact of his talking with her was more important than the content.

As the days passed she found the regular routine of ward activities distracted her mind from Alison's problems. The gradually lengthening evenings seemed to offer more time for the patients to spend in the music-room. She had found a slightly larger audience during her Bach practice sessions, and the staff did not hurry the patients off to bed after evening drinks. She was surprised to see Fred occasionally join the small band of listeners. He was the last person she would expect to enjoy such music, but she was rapidly learning not to be surprised at anything the patients might do.

This learning was tested when Tracey appeared at the sing-song session with three ladies in tow. 'We've been invited, Caroline. Can we join your musical evenings?'

Caroline grinned at her friend. She knew Tracey's bubbling personality would be more than helpful during the singing and she stole a quick look at Bob, who was seated in a back row. They now had twelve regular male singers and the three women would be a welcome addition.

It took her a short time to single out which new addition was Bob's special friend, but it seemed to be a slight, thin woman who smiled shyly at him as he offered to share his copy of the song sheets.

Tracey was turning the pages for Caroline and whispered, 'That's our Gladys.'

Caroline looked at her friend with wide eyes. The shop-lifting expert? Tracey winked and nodded slightly, then raised her voice to belt out a chorus of 'My Old Man'.

Towards the end of the week Bob's lady-friend approached Caroline and asked if she could make a request.

'Of course, Gladys. What would you like to sing?'

'This.'

Caroline looked down at the well-worn sheet music the small woman put in her hand. It was Mozart's *Ave Verum*. 'Oh, this *is* very beautiful music, but I don't think. . .' Caroline doubted if her enthusiastic but amateur group could cope with the intricacies of the little woman's choice.

'It's really not that difficult, Nurse. My church choir sang it and if we could do it, anyone can.' She seemed quite sure of herself and Caroline was not prepared to dampen any patient's enthusiasm.

'All right, Gladys. We'll have a go. I'll get photocopies of the parts and we'll see what we can do.'

The group's response to the first attempt to sing the harmonies of Mozart was a surprise to Caroline. She had underestimated the patients' enjoyment and ability to hear what they were singing. For the first time they had great music to sing and they began to learn to make music themselves. Caroline wondered what she had started; there would be no stopping them now. They asked her for more time to learn their parts and she had to divide them up into groups. Gladys brought more women over from Whitney and Caroline found herself trying to organise the direction of a twenty-voice choir.

She laughed with Meg in the office after two weeks of attempting to co-ordinate the activities of all the patients, 'I'll be relieved to get back to days. I thought evenings would be quieter!'

The ward sister smiled at her. 'It's good to have so much activity going on here. Folkestone is getting a good reputation and I know a few other wards are quite envious. Has David told you what he's planning?'

'No.' Caroline smiled. She had not seen him other than on the ward but was content enough to know he was around. Tracey had mentioned that he had taken over the weekend duties of another registrar covering the long-term units and Caroline accepted that his work would always be a priority.

Meg's cheerful voice interrupted her thoughts. 'He's thinking we will put on a performance!' She chuckled softly.

'Oh, no,' Caroline groaned. She was very proud of her troupe of singers but doubted they could face an audience.

'Oh, yes. He's had Eric build some sort of stage and he thinks we can charge ten pence each for people who want to come. We could use the petty cash, I'll admit to that.' Meg grinned at her.

Sure enough, the following day Eric and Bob arrived in the music room, carrying their tools and piles of planks, and started to construct what looked like a short platform at the end of the long room. Caroline made admiring comments on their work, but doubted if her choir could deal with a public performance.

Again, she had underestimated the patients' enthusiasm. As they started to rehearse that evening, Eric was their first 'outside' listener. After Bob joined the singers—always beside Gladys—Eric stopped his work and, at the end of their music-hall medley, applauded with hearty approval.

'This is good! Very good. I like it.' He was smiling and nodding.

'Just wait, Eric. We're doing Gladys's song next. It's the best.' Bob turned around and hushed Eric with authority, at which the OT supervisor raised his eyebrows with delight. Bob had never given him directions before and Eric was well pleased with this sign of independence.

Caroline shuffled the group around so that the voices would blend more evenly and, as she turned to the piano, she was surprised to see Anton Vanijek move to the chair before her.

'It is better you direct. Perhaps I can play. . .?' He bent his head slightly in a question.

'Of course, Mr Vanijek. I would be very grateful.' Caroline was thrilled. He had usually sat as a quiet observer but had shown no interest in participation. She didn't doubt that he could play the music.

As his slender hands quietly began the opening bars, Caroline felt tiny goose-bumps go up her spine. The man was a great musician and he was playing with the interpretation Mozart had intended. The soft intensity of his touch seemed to fill the room. As she silently gave the downbeat and heard the first blend of their voices, she knew the patients had also heard his skill. For the first time they sang with intensity and power, the music soaring above and beyond them. Every face was fastened on her hands and face and they followed each direction with certainty. They could hear themselves and their pride overflowed into the finest singing she had ever heard from them.

They finished in absolute unison and Caroline could say nothing. She just beamed at them all, her pleasure and pride obvious. She wanted to hug every one of them and tell them what wonderful music they had made.

Eric was applauding with great force. 'This is wonderful! Wonderful! And you, Mr Vanijek, sir. Wonderful, wonderful!' He was clapping his hands and he bowed his head towards the quietly smiling musician.

'Yes. Thank you, Mr Vanijek.' Caroline looked at him, willing him the accept the praise of others.

'I think perhaps, in bar thirty. . .the men were too slow to come in. . .' He played the passage and Caroline laughed.

'All right, Mr Vanijek, we will go over it again.' He was quite correct and, although she would not have demanded such perfection, she would follow his critical judgement. His high standards of musicianship were a sign of health in him and she knew how important her support could be.

This was a turning-point for the singing group and

they became more serious about their rehearsal times. They knew they would be expected to perform and gradually a regular repertoire emerged. They had included Mr Lawrence's 'Tipperary' and Caroline suspected that during the Mozart the tone-deaf Mr Lawrence simply mouthed the words. She certainly couldn't hear his distinctive breathy voice during the *Ave Verum* and she mentally gave thanks for the old man's wisdom. The *Ave* had become the group's showpiece and Anton Vanijek continued to be their accompanist.

One evening as she was working on a complex Bach prelude, with Mr Vanijek as a supportive audience of one, they were interrupted by the quiet entrance of Eric. Caroline saw the box he was carrying and made a move to leave.

'No, Nurse, please stay.' Eric motioned with his hand and she remained seated, watching attentively. 'Sir. . .' he turned to the musician '. . .if you please, I. . .' His voice stopped and he took a deep breath. 'This is something I wish you to have. It is yours.'

With a quick gesture he thrust the box on to Anton Vanijek's lap. 'It is not what you are used to, I know. But it is yours.'

As Eric stood with his hands clasped tightly in front of his waist, the musician slowly opened the box and lifted the towelling. As Anton Vanijek saw the contents, his head bowed low so that the watchers could not see his face. One fine, slender hand carefully traced the carving and lightly touched a single string.

Caroline watched in anxious silence and her breathing stopped briefly as he closed the lid after carefully replacing the covering. Eric must have worked very hard to finish his work on the violin and Caroline could feel her own tension. Surely the patient could not refuse such a gift.

The musician slowly stood up and, holding the closed box, spoke to Eric in a language Caroline could not understand. His words sounded very serious and solemn, but she saw Eric smile. As she continued to watch silently, Anton Vanijek bowed slightly to Eric and turned to say his usual polite thanks to her, 'As always, a pleasure, Nurse.'

As he left the room, walking very slowly, with the box tucked under his arm, Caroline turned to Eric. 'Is it all right?'

'I think so. I hope so.' Eric smiled quietly. 'He accepts it, so no more can I ask.'

Caroline could only hope that the musician understood the pride and respect that had produced the lovely instrument.

On the ward Caroline noted that Mr Vanijek was being included in other activities with the patients and he no longer sat alone in the dining-room. The nursing reports included records of his eating regular meals, small in quantity but enough to avoid the necessity of increasing his medication. This patient did seem to be making a slow recovery.

Martin had also progressed, as he joined Terry on one of the small drums. Terry had produced two small wooden hollow gourds that made a sound like hoofbeats and Martin thoroughly enjoyed tapping them under Terry's watchful guidance. Their percussion section had been augmented by the appearance of Winston, carrying a small leather-covered drum that he beat with a soft, insistent rhythm. But it was Mr Lawrence's tissue-covered comb that caused Caroline to break out laughing.

'What on earth have you got there?' She went over to see how he produced the thin reedy sound under his cupped hands. He showed her his comb with a mischievous grin.

'Old ways is the best ways, Nurse.' He gave a wheezy chuckle and demonstrated the range of his skills, to the clapping laughter of the other patients. They were developing a fair range of sounds, although the Mozart remained accompanied only by the piano.

She knew from Annabelle and Tracey that the news of the Folkestone group had spread through the hospital. In the afternoon art group held on Wednesdays, the non-singing members of the ward group had been set to drawing posters advertising the concert which was set for the end of the month.

At the end of one of the ward meetings David had suggested the title 'February Folkestone Follies' for their performance and, as she smiled at him, Caroline noticed the dark rings under his eyes. She thought he was probably working too hard. He seemed to be losing his deep tan, but she brushed her slight worry aside. If he was taking care of private patients as well as all his Castleview responsibilities, that was his business. Still, she couldn't help thinking about him.

She continued her morning bicycle rides, sometimes to the village, carefully avoiding the old farmhouse. She would not seek him out. Learning patience was difficult, but she could wait. She would have to be satisfied with the lovely dreams that filtered through her sleep after she fell exhausted into bed after every late shift.

The musical group was augmented by yet more eager participants one evening, when Andrew arrived with four of his patients straggling behind him. Caroline grinned at him—he looked so pleased with himself. She suspected it had taken some effort to get his patients actually over to Folkestone, but she didn't know how her cohesive group would take to the inclusion of strangers.

'Hi, Caroline. We've come to join. Hey, Ernie, keep those trousers up!' Andrew pulled up the sagging trousers of a round young man who was smiling and nodding happily, with apparent disregard for the state of his clothing.

'Hello, Andrew.' Caroline's doubt sounded in her voice.

'We can sing, all right. Really. . .here, Janice, let's show them.' Andrew took the hand of a very short, tubby woman with her hair tied in two pony-tails and wearing a frilled flowered skirt. 'Sing "Bye Bye Blackbird" for us.'

It seemed Janice felt suddenly shy and she shook her head, giggling.

'Come on, Janice,' Andrew was encouraging, 'you can do it. I know you can.'

Caroline suddenly realised that Andrew had probably spent a great deal of time teaching his small group so they could join in and she smiled at Janice. Caroline took the woman's hand and led her over to the piano. Before she could play the opening notes for her, a booming voice interrupted them.

'March, march, march!' This was another of Andrew's patients, a large young man with a face-splitting grin who was energetically lifting and dropping his feet in one spot. 'We can march!'

'Well, yes, Denny, we can march all right, but I'm not sure that's what these people want.' Andrew looked over at Caroline and shrugged his shoulders.

'If you like. . .' Caroline glanced at Terry who nodded and started to tap out a light six-eight rhythm. Immediately all of Andrew's patients started on the move. They were happily picking up their feet and swinging their arms in perfect time to the beat.

As she watched their obvious pleasure, Caroline grinned to see Mr Lawrence start to march behind them, tooting on his home-made instrument. She was suddenly astounded by a loud crashing chord behind her back. She whirled to see Anton Vanijek seated at the piano, smiling broadly.

At her unbelieving look, his eyes twinkled as he started to pound out a familiar melody with forceful emphasis. Caroline listened astonished as the martial sounds of the Radetzky March burst from the small piano. She wondered if Osbert could stand the strain as the pianist was certainly not holding back. He was ripping into the music and Terry and Martin leapt to join the vigorous rhythm matching each thundering beat.

Caroline glanced over at Terry and was rewarded with the sight of the boy's complete concentration on Mr Vanijek's movements. He was certainly following musical direction and obviously having no difficulty accepting the authority of Anton Vanijek. She looked over at the rest of the patients.

The joyful enthusiasm of the music had been impossible for them to resist and she laughed to see all her hard
working choristers bouncing along in the wake of
Andrew's marching trio. Trio? As she looked around for
the missing patient, she heard Andrew call from across
the room.

'Caroline! Get Janice! She's over there.' He was firmly
holding on to the unreliable trousers of his lead marcher
as he waved in a direction across the room.

Janice was happily stomping around in circles by
herself in a corner of the room and Caroline ran over to
bring her back to the moving line now curling around
the centre of the room. Andrew and Ernie were leading
the marchers up the steps of the improvised stage and
back down again.

The thumping chords were echoed by booming bangs
from the drums. As Mr Vanijek made a swift downward
hand movement Terry responded immediately; the
music softened to a gentle regular rocking rhythm. The
marching patients crept on tiptoe with exaggerated
movements and Caroline was reminded of a group of
nursery school children in a playground.

Another quick hand movement, Terry gave a loud
drum roll and they all resumed their exuberant march.
Holding tightly to Janice's hand, Caroline tried to find
Andrew and, as she looked around, she saw David and
Meg watching from the doorway. They were both smil-
ing broadly.

'You've started something here, my lad.' Meg's delight
was obvious.

'So it would seem. From the sounds of this, I'll have
to hire the Albert Hall next.' He was watching the
laughing girl hanging on to the rotund marching patient.

Meg gave him a small push in the back, 'Go on, my
boy. Join the fun. You could use the relaxation!'

With a short laugh, David strolled towards the now
tiring marchers and grinned over at Anton Vanijek. He
made a small thumbs-up sign at the musician who
nodded back and, with a flourish of arpeggios, rounded
off the music with a grand series of repeated crashing
chords.

The patients finished with breathless laughter and a few just sat down where they were, in a tumbled heap. Caroline helped Mr Lawrence to a chair; he was certainly wheezing, and she looked at the flushed faces of Martin and Terry over on the drums. Both boys looked very proud of themselves and were applauding everyone's efforts.

'Hey, Anton, that was great stuff!' Terry's enthusiastic approval did not seem inappropriate and Caroline smiled to herself. She wondered if the great musician had ever been complimented in quite that way before.

His smiling 'Thank you, Terence. You also played well,' brought a surprised grin to the boy's face.

'Excellent, Mr Vanijek. You've worn everyone out.' David touched the smiling pianist lightly on the shoulder.

'My pleasure.' Anton Vanijek nodded his response. 'You did not march with the others, Doctor?'

'No, I arrived a little late for that.' David looked at him thoughtfully. 'I don't suppose you could provide something a little less energetic for us tired old staff?'

The grey eyes looked up at the young face and a slow smile spread across the aristocratic features. 'Ah, perhaps. . .a little lighter in tempo, a little more gentle?' As he talked, he was fingering the keys with a flowing touch.

Caroline did not hear the conversation, but she certainly heard the music. Now he was beginning a slow waltz. She couldn't name it but it came from a bygone world in distant times and spoke of elegance and romance. Her mind became filled with visions of gleaming candelabra reflecting the sheen of shimmering jewels and rich fabrics swaying to the carefree strains of the lyrical melody.

Her dreaming thoughts were interrupted by a warm voice. 'Miss Caroline, may I have the honour of this dance?'

She looked up to see David Hunter with an expression of exaggerated entreaty on his face. She tilted her head slightly, as if to consider his request, then smiled and held out her hand.

He promptly bent his head over with a precise bow

and kissed her fingers with the briefest brush of his lips. Before she could regain possession of her hand, Caroline found herself firmly encircled within strong arms that threatened to sweep her off her feet.

David held her lightly around the waist and led her with authority in a slow, circular sweep around the room.

Caroline looked up at the formally erect head. 'You are a good dancer!'

'Your tone of surprise is most discourteous, Miss Caroline.' He turned her quickly in a swift swirl and grinned down at her. 'One of the useful advantages of a posh education, my dear. I will have you know that I am also aware of what a fish fork looks like.'

She stifled a giggle and glanced over his shoulder. She could see Bob and Gladys decorously circling at the far end of the room. A heavy stomping sound caused her to turn her head, just in time to see Andrew bounding by, his hands firmly clasping a chortling Janice. Their steps seemed to ressemble a polka more than a waltz, but they both looked delighted with their efforts.

'Look at Andrew!' She watched the energetic couple narrowly miss a stack of chairs.

'I have no wish to look at Andrew or anyone else.' He looked down at her face, his mouth curved with tenderness.

Caroline could feel her cheeks flush slightly, 'David. . .we're at work!'

'You may be. I'm not.' His arm tightened around her waist and he pulled her closer to his side. 'I'm in a gold and silver ballroom with crystal chandeliers reflected in a thousand mirrors. The orchestra is playing and my lady love is sparkling with diamonds in her hair and smells deliciously of summer lilac.' He sniffed the air. 'Yes, I think it's definitely lilac.'

'More likely hospital disinfectant,' Caroline muttered as she tried to follow the increasing intricacy of his steps.

David gave an exaggerated sigh. 'Ah, the tribulations of loving an earth-bound creature. Careful now, here comes the tricky bit—on the downbeat, we dip.' As he suited actions to words, Caroline's mind whirled with the music and their movements.

Love? He had said loving. What was he saying? What did he mean? She had no time to think or react as they twirled and swayed to the lilting rhythm. She could only submit to the firmness of the arms holding her and follow wherever he chose to lead.

The world had become a private space bound by their two bodies moving in unison. As she responded to each light pressure on her hand and waist, Caroline felt herself becoming weightless and she closed her eyes to float on a gossamer cloud of pure happiness. David was quite right. They were surrounded by shimmering reflections, gleaming marble floors and elegant women in extravagant ball gowns gracefully spinning in the arms of handsome men, but not one of them as handsome as. . .

'There he is! There! I told you!'

A voice was shouting with fury and reverberated around the room. The music suddenly stopped.

As she turned towards the door, Caroline felt David's arm tighten briefly on her waist as he muttered 'Damnation' under his breath. Before she could make sense of what she was seeing, David had begun to move towards the red-faced man.

It was Fred, and he was brandishing an object above his head. Behind him stood a worried-looking Eric and one of the hospital security men.

'What seems to be the problem, Fred?' David's voice was calm and conversational as he approached the threesome. All of the patients were motionless and silent, watching the tableau before them.

'There! He took my watch! He did it! We found it. And I want him! He's your thief!' Fred was blustering with rage, his face a vivid shade of purple, and he was now pointing an accusatory finger directly at Terry.

It was Anton Vanijek who broke the stunned silence the shouted outburst had caused.

'I believe you must be mistaken, sir. Terence is no thief.' He had risen from the piano and stood quietly, with one hand placed lightly on the drum behind which Terry was standing. The boy stood absolutely still, only the whitened knuckles gripping the sticks he still held betrayed any reaction to Fred's entrance.

'There's no mistake! I know——'

'That's enough, Fred.' David cut across the belligerent voice.

'I'm sorry, Doctor.' Eric had stepped forward, obviously unhappy at Fred's behaviour. 'We *did* find the wristwatch in Terry's workbench drawer. . .' He looked over at Terry with an apologetic smile. 'I'm sure there is a reasonable explanation. . .'

'Yes, I'm sure——' David was quietly agreeing with the supervisor, but this time he was interrupted.

Fred's voice cut like a jagged knife through the calm of David's words. 'It was there, all right! Everybody saw it! I want my fiver back, and where did you put the kettle, then, eh?' He had moved forward and was glaring at Terry, waving the watch in front of his face.

Caroline watched the blood drain from the boy's face as he kept his eyes on Fred. Everyone in the room had turned to look at Terry and the clenched fist inches from his nose, holding the shiny wristwatch.

Just as David uttered a quiet 'steady, lad,' Terry threw down the sticks with a loud clatter on the largest drum and dashed for the exit, brushing past Fred and evading Eric's instinctively outstretched hand.

Everyone seemed to be frozen to the spot as his running footsteps were heard echoing down the corridor, quickly fading to a deathly silence.

CHAPTER TEN

THE blank expression on Terry's pale face haunted Caroline's mind as she joined Meg in settling the patients after Fred's outburst. Andrew had quietly taken his patients back to their ward and David had disappeared. Somehow Caroline knew that he would try to follow Terry so the boy could not disappear alone. If anyone could help him, she knew David could. She had wanted to run after him, but realised that her work was with the others, many of whom were very upset.

She helped Mr Lawrence to bed after getting him a hot drink, and went to look for Martin. He had retreated to his room and she stood at the door, looking at his hunched form seated on the small bed.

'Are you all right, Martin?' She could see the two wooden gourds on the chair beside his bed; she knew he had been developing a friendship with Terry and wasn't sure how he would react to the verbal attack. Caroline remained standing in the doorway, relieved to note her own lack of anxiety with Martin.

He lifted his head and his black eyes showed only confusion and sadness. 'Why did he do that?'

Caroline could not believe that Terry would ever steal anything from anyone and she trusted Martin to believe the same. 'Do you mean Fred?'

'Yeah. He had no call to yell like that.'

'No, he didn't.' Explaining Fred's behaviour was a problem. She had felt her own anger at the aggressive man, but Martin genuinely needed to understand. She wasn't sure she did herself.

Caroline thought for a moment. 'Perhaps Fred has difficulty controlling his temper. You know, he has complained a lot about losing things.' As she spoke, she tried to see Fred in a different light, from his point of view. 'It's hard to live here in the hospital. You know that too, don't you?'

She accepted his nod and spoke slowly, 'And possessions are important—especially if you don't have very much else to hold on to. When you lose something,' she thought of David's information about Martin's broken relationship, 'sometimes it can seem much more important to you than it seems to anyone else.'

His eyes were fastened on her face and again he nodded, slowly. She continued, 'Fred thought he knew who had taken his possessions and he wanted to attack.' She looked at Martin's attentive face. 'I'm sure he regrets it now, but it was his first reaction. He is probably sorry for what he did. . .' Caroline could only hope she was

right; she remembered Fred's look of shocked surprise
as Terry had rushed past him out of the room.

'Yeah.' Martin nodded again and paused before looking at her with a solemn expression. 'I'm sorry I grabbed
at you, Nurse. I didn't mean——'

Caroline smiled at him. 'I know, Martin. And I'm
sorry I hit you with the spoon. You startled me, and I
guess I acted a bit like Fred. My first reaction was to
strike out.' It felt good to be able to say this to him.

Martin gave her a lop-sided smile, 'You didn't half
thump me one!' He rubbed his ear ,thoughtfully.
'Haven't felt anything like that since me mum gave me a
clip on the ear!'

Caroline smiled, relieved that he had accepted some
explanation for unpredictable behaviour, at least her
own.

There was no news of Terry's whereabouts by the time
she left the ward at the end of her shift. He had not
turned up at home and David was busy on the telephone,
informing various services, including Gillian, to use the
community networks to trace him. He answered
Caroline's quick question with a shake of the head when
she asked if he was contacting the police. She sighed,
hoping that Terry wouldn't do himself too much damage
this time.

The residence building was quiet when she went up to
her room, again feeling drained by her work. She soaked
in a hot bath and was feeling too drowsy to read or work
on her case study, even though she would be able to add
an account of Martin's development in self-understand-
ing. As well as my own, she thought tiredly.

A soft knock on the door prevented her from burrow-
ing deep into her bed and she heard Andrew's voice.
'Caroline. Are you still up?'

'Just a minute.' Putting on her robe, Caroline opened
the door. 'Hi, Andrew. How are your people? Did they
settle all right?'

He nodded. 'Oh, yes. They don't get very upset at
noise and commotion. They think it's all part of the fun.
There is something else I wanted to tell you. About
Alison.'

'Oh.' She opened the door widely and hurriedly removed her piled clothing from the chair. 'Come on in, Andrew. I was too tired to work, but I think my mind is too busy to sleep. What's happened?'

'They found them. Ben is back with his family and I guess Alison is as well.' He sat down heavily. 'She won't be coming back, which I suppose is no surprise.'

'Poor Alison.' Caroline perched on her bed. 'I'm going to miss her. I thought she was doing so well. I still think she would have been a good psych nurse.'

Andrew nodded. 'No chance now. I wonder if she'll be allowed to keep her general registration?' They sat in silence for a moment.

'Where did she take Ben?' asked Caroline.

'They went up to a theme park—one of those places with activities for kids—under a glass bubble in a forest somewhere. She just booked them in for a week's holiday.' Andrew shrugged sadly. 'Fantasy-time, all of it. Pure fantasy.'

'Do you think she intended to bring him back?' Caroline knew she was holding on to some remnant of her belief in Alison.

'Who knows? It doesn't really matter. She had no idea that what she was doing was wrong. None at all.'

Caroline muttered under her breath. 'No anchovies.'

'Sorry? I didn't hear what you said.' Andrew lifted his head.

She shuffled her feet slightly, 'I was just thinking of something someone said about mixing the childlike need for play with a sense of what's right and wrong.'

'Well, somebody forgot to teach Alison, that's for sure.' He stood up slowly. 'I'll miss her too. I liked her.' He added thoughtfully, 'I still do. I just hope she finds a place where she can fit in and be happy.' He turned with his hand on the doorknob. 'You seem to be happy, Caroline. Is this a place where you fit in?'

'Yes. Yes, I think it is. And you?' She smiled broadly at him, hoping he shared her feelings about Castleview.

'I'm beginning to. I wasn't sure when I started, but it seems there is a place for me here, too. See you.' He grinned at her and gently closed her door.

Caroline snuggled down to sleep, slightly comforted by Andrew's satisfaction with this kind of nursing.

During her bicycle ride the following morning, Caroline deliberately went down to the village. She stopped at the restaurant, not knowing if she should say anything to Mr Mapley. She had no wish to intrude, but if there had been news of Terry's whereabouts, surely they would know. The doors and windows were firmly closed and she decided to leave unobtrusively. As she turned, she noticed an ancient estate wagon chugging down the village road. It was the vicar, and this time he was driving himself.

He stopped, with a clanking of gears, outside the restaurant. 'Good morning, Nurse.' He smiled at her.

'Good morning, Vicar.' She was surprised he remembered her, and risked a question, as she wondered about the cause of his visit to Terry's home. Something could have happened.

'Do you have any news. . .of Terry, I mean?' She paused and then added hastily, 'He's on my ward and I was wondering. . .?'

'Not much, dear. We heard he's gone down to the coast and it seems he is safe.' He nodded at her and knocked on the restaurant door.

'Thank you. I'm glad he's all right.' Caroline wheeled her bicycle away before the door opened. She did not want to appear to be overly curious and the family was entitled to privacy. Still, it seemed Terry was safe, at least.

She hurried on to the ward later and mentioned her news to Meg, following the staff report. Terry had not been mentioned and the patients all appeared to be somewhat subdued during the morning activities.

'Yes, I know, Caroline. You'll find David in the staff-room, if you want to talk to him.' The ward sister's tone of voice was calm, but Caroline thought she could detect an undertone of anxiety and she quickly went through to the coffee-room.

David was seated, with his head propped up by a bent elbow. He does look tired, thought Caroline. He really doesn't need this extra worry on top of everything else he has to do. She sat down beside him quietly.

He raised his head and smiled warmly. 'Oh, hello, Caro. Been dozing a bit, I'm afraid. The caffeine zap doesn't seem to be working any more.'

'You need something more than coffee.' Caroline wished she could do more to help him.

His blue eyes twinkled at her as he grinned mischievously. 'And just what were you suggesting, my beautiful sparrow?'

She blushed and wrinkled her nose at him. 'A proper meal and some decent sleep was what I was thinking of.'

'That will come eventually. Just two more overtime shifts and I'll be finished.' He looked around for his missing coffee-mug. Caroline went over to the cupboard and took out a large bowl.

'If you can sit for a minute, I'll make you some soup. We always have something stashed away for the patients.' As she plugged in the kettle and hunted for the small supply of tinned goods, she added, in what she hoped was a casual tone of voice, 'Why all the overtime? I thought you might be occupied with your private patients.'

A soft chuckle greeted her question. 'I had a small bank overdraft to repay and the overtime was needed for financial reasons. And no, the private patient business has gone into a sudden decline—along with the patient, I'm afraid.' His voice had taken on a more serious tone and Caroline looked at him, stopping briefly as she tussled with the tin opener.

'Did something happen to that patient you went to see?'

'Hmm. I have removed myself from the case, in a manner of speaking.' He shrugged lightly and sniffed as the faint aroma of vegetable soup began to rise from the saucepan Caroline was stirring. 'Ah. . .the elixir of life.'

She laughed, 'Hardly, but it is better than your constant infusions of coffee.' She hunted around for crackers, but had to settle for some tea biscuits.

She watched as he tasted the soup, nodded his satisfaction and tucked into it. Sitting across from him, with her

arms folded on the table, Caroline had a sudden image
of them seated this way for the rest of their lives—in
their own kitchen with the lovely smells of home cooking
in the air. She smiled at her own dreaminess. There were
more practical realities to be dealt with, and they were
sitting in the middle of a psychiatric admission ward, not
a rose-covered cottage in the country.

'Have you heard about Terry? The vicar said he had
gone to the coast.' She remembered the worry in Meg's
voice.

'Yes.' He finished the soup with a satisfied pat of his
abdomen. 'Thank you, Caro. Hit the spot. I've been a
bit short of the daily nutritional requirements lately.' He
responded to her question with a brief lowering of his
had. 'Gillian and her trusty telephone found him, in a
local hospital on the coast.'

Caroline looked up, startled, 'In a hospital? He cut
himself again, then?'

David nodded. 'Only this time he used a broken bottle
he picked up on the beach. A clean razor would have
been preferable, if he has to do it at all.'

Caroline sighed. Poor Terry. She wondered if he
would ever learn any other way of dealing with difficult
feelings. His self-mutilation seemed to be a vicious circle
of behaviour impossible to break.

David began to shift his weight away from the table,
with reluctant slowness. 'No way around it. Must get
back to the sick and needy.' He looked over at her. 'How
is your physical strength these days?'

She raised her eyebrows. 'As much as can be expected,
I suppose. Why?' She wasn't going to volunteer for
anything without knowing what he was talking about.

'I'm about to move—from the farmhouse into the
village. I could use some help with the packing, if not
the actual heaving and lifting.' He had kept a watchful
eye on the off-duty roster and knew she had this weekend
off.

'Moving?' Caroline felt a tiny lurch of her heart.
'Where are you going?'

'A colleague is moving out of a flat over the chemist's
shop and I've taken over the lease. It's small, but

enough, and not much further from the hospital.' He grinned. 'The chemist is delighted to have a medical resource on the premises; apparently occupancy includes an unofficial on-call duty to the local pharmacist.'

'That sounds lovely.' Caroline felt her spirits lift. 'I'd like to help if I can, but I had planned to go up to see my aunt on Saturday.'

As he stood up, David looked down at her. 'Ah, yes. I wanted to talk to you about that. Can I pick you up on Saturday morning? I actually have this weekend clear, for once.'

'All right.' Caroline was puzzled. Why should he want to talk about her aunt? She was slightly uneasy at his glance, but she shrugged it off. She would find out soon enough, and the prospect of a weekend away from the patients and their troubles was something to look forward to. Being with David again was a secret pleasure to be treasured.

She worked hard on her case study that was due the following week, and, when checking the calendar, was surprised to see that she had completed over half her time on Folkestone. It was going to be difficult to leave all the patients.

She still sat at the piano during the hour after the supper period, but the ladies no longer came over from Whitney, except Gladys who occasionally came to sit with Bob. The patients would listen to her play but few actually sang. As if by mutual consent, the choir did not rehearse their performance repertoire; the plans for a performance had been silently shelved. They all missed Terry and were aware of where he was. It was as if they were waiting for him to return before they could carry on as they had been.

Caroline realised that the choir had become a strong group with an identity of its own, and the lack of one important member left a feeling of loss. She played any music they requested and continued to practise her Bach. Several patients would wander in and out, although Mr Vanijek had·become a regular listener.

One evening he came alone, after the evening drinks, and he was carrying Eric's violin. Caroline made no

comment, but continued to play a Bach fugue that had
been giving her considerable difficulty. As she had
hoped, Mr Vanijek slowly tuned the strings with her
help and started on a soft version of the major harmony.
They were both hesitant and uncertain,' but Caroline
could hear the expert's ear in the sounds he made on the
violin. It was as if the musician was retuning the rusty
instrument of his own skill. At other times he came only
to listen, and always politely thanked her when he left.

Saturday morning arrived as a day warming up to a
proper spring. Caroline opened one eye when a sliver of
sunlight crept through the slit in her curtains. It was an
unusual experience—being wakened by a bright light in
the morning. She sighed and stretched languidly. Perhaps the winter would finally be forced to give way to
spring.

After ten straight days on duty she revelled in the joy
of having two whole days to herself. To herself and
David. She laughed lightly. Wondering what a flat over
a chemist's shop would look like, she quickly dressed in
what she considered to be her working clothes—freshly
laundered jeans and a thick woolly jumper with a zig-zag
pattern of blue and white stripes. It was worth a chance
to leave her jacket behind; it might be warm enough,
especially if she was going to have to shift furniture
around.

Caroline was sitting on the front steps, lifting her face
to the slight warmth of the sun, when she saw an old
battered van from the village draw up. She clambered
up on the high seat with an energetic bounce.

'You seem to be in fine form this morning,' David's
warm gaze swept swiftly over her casual clothing, 'and
as beautiful as always.'

Caroline laughed and coloured slightly, under the
intensity of his look. 'This is my removal-gang costume.
Do you intend to fill this van?'

'I already have. It took all night to pack up my humble
goods and chattels. After so many nights awake, one
more didn't seem to make any difference.' He was
turning around in a wide arc and swerved to miss a bent

figure, shuffling along the main entrance to the administration building. 'Whoops, nearly got old Charlie there. Heaven only knows where he's off to now.'

Caroline twisted around in her seat to get a look at the rarely seen porter, but she missed him as they turned to leave the grounds. She still didn't know what he looked like, and she wondered if she would ever see him, with or without the pharmacy box.

'Any news of Terry?' Caroline watched the now familiar road to the village unfold in front of them. It was certainly faster in a car than on a bicycle, and she could see further across the fields. There seemed to be a vague greening of the land and she sniffed the air.

'No, nothing new.' He glanced quickly over at her. 'Definitely things happening here though. Buds are budding and the grass is rising. . .' He started to hum lightly.

'Maybe we'll get an early spring. I saw crocus shoots at the vicar's house last month.' Listening to herself, Caroline had an odd sensation that she had done all this before. It was a strange feeling, as if she had been sitting high up in this van in some other life and had said and felt everything she was saying and feeling right now. She smiled happily. It seemed as if she was meant to be here and that everything was going according to some grand plan.

Caroline was surprised when David slowed and parked in front of the chemist's shop at the near end of the village. She had been lost in her own thoughts and she looked up at the first-floor windows. They were dirt-speckled and curtainless. Immediately her imagination had them sparkling clean and showing warm colours of soft curtains.

She jumped down and started to carry small cartons up the stairs, following David. They were small boxes, but heavy. Books, she thought; trust me to pick the deceptive-looking ones. They climbed up and down until all the boxes had been dumped in the small sitting-room, and then Caroline had a chance to look around.

It was a very compact flat, with a sitting-room at the end of the corridor, facing the street. There were two tiny bedrooms—'boxrooms' according to David—a kitchen barely large enough for a table and a small bathroom.

'Not much, but mine own.' David was attempting to work the small gas cooker. 'Hah. Persistence pays off.' He placed a kettle full of water on the flame. 'Now for the furnishings.'

Caroline watched him with curiosity. He didn't seem to have any furniture that she could see. She followed him into the sitting-room and watched as he piled empty cartons and boxes into an odd arrangement.

'This is an easy chair,' he pointed to a double-length set of turned-over cartons, 'and this is, of course, the sofa.' He placed four cartons end to end and stretched out on his back. 'A trifle hard, but manageable.'

She laughed as he turned his head. 'Is this where you intend to sleep?'

'No, I have a couple of sleeping-bags and a camp-bed. Quite comfortable, really.' He slowly drew himself upright. 'Better than this sofa, I think.'

She remembered that he must have a fair amount of skiing and mountain climbing gear, with camping equipment. He was probably quite accustomed to sleeping on the ground. As she looked around, she tried to picture the little room as it might be, but her imagination was limited by the sad state of the walls and flooring. She sighed lightly. Having curtains seemed to be the least of his worries. He needed everything.

'It's not that bad.' David had stood up and, standing behind her, put his arm around her shoulders. Caroline felt the warmth of him and resisted the urge to lean back against his solidity. She felt a light touch on the top of her head, but before she could react he had quickly retreated to remove the whistling kettle from the cooker.

He returned with two mugs of tea. 'No milk, I'm afraid, but at least it's hot.' He placed her mug next to the 'chair' and sat cross-legged on the floor. 'I'll have to nip out and get some provisions, including a couple of pots of paint, I think. What colour do you fancy?'

Preferring the safety of the firm floor to the uncertain stability of the cartons, Caroline joined him on the floor.

So he wanted her to help decorate. She looked around speculatively. He probably wanted bright yellow walls with pink stripes, if his taste in sports clothes was any indication. Well, he could have a yellow kitchen. That would be nice.

'Mushroom?' she suggested tentatively.

David laughed out loud. 'I should have known! The sparrow will want browns.' He glinted at her. 'And what else? Can't have everything brown. How about a little bit of red?'

'No! No red!' The exclamation burst out of her and she laughed at his expression. She tried to explain, 'I'm not really very fond of red. But blue would be nice—different shades of blues and browns.'

He grinned at her. 'Earth colours.' He looked around at the grubby walls. 'Well, that might do—earth and sky. It will depend on the local supplies, I'm afraid.'

Caroline looked at her watch. It was nearly noon. 'I really must go, David. I wanted to catch a train up to London, to see my aunt. What did you want to say about her?'

'Ah.' He sat upright and looked at her. 'There is something I have to tell you.' He paused. 'I haven't told you before because I wasn't sure. . .' He looked down at his mug thoughtfully. 'I didn't know if what I did would make any difference.'

'What you did? What have you done?' Caroline felt a sense of irritation. What had he to do with Aunt Betty? He had only seen her once.

David looked at her seriously. 'When I was with your aunt, I had my doubts as to whether she was suffering from any form of dementia. She recognised you and she was responding physiologically to everything you said. She also responded quite appropriately to my presence. There was no agitation or confusion that I could detect. But I could be wrong. . .'

Caroline held her breath. She had always had a secret wish that her aunt was not senile. Was he saying that she was not? Then what was wrong with her?

His voice was continuing, 'So I referred her to Edward Staveley at the Heathfield.' Before she could interrupt, he spoke quickly, 'I phoned him after our visit and asked him to go and see her. If he thought she might benefit from some tests, he would take her on, as a diagnostic problem. He's very interested in such difficult cases.'

'Dr Staveley?' Caroline swallowed her astonishment. 'You referred Aunt Betty to him? At the Heathfield?' She was beginning to feel more irritated at David's high-handedness. He could at least have asked her opinion, without barging ahead on his own, without so much as a by-your-leave!

'Yes, I did. I'm sorry, Caroline, if you disapprove. But I wasn't sure if my intuition was correct. And I trust his judgement. If he said she was not organically ill, then my decision would be justified.'

'And did he?' Caroline suppressed her growing anger as she held her breath for his answer.

'Yes. He says he hasn't found any indication for a diagnosis of dementia,' David answered.

'What has he found, then?' She could hear the hope mixed with irritation in her own voice.

'I think you will need to talk to him about that.' David kept his voice quiet.

'Haven't you been speaking with him?' She couldn't believe that he would take such action without following through. He had just removed Aunt Betty from her comfortable nursing home and had put her into an acute psychiatric unit. She well knew how good the Heathfield unit was, but the change must have been upsetting.

'Yes, I've spoken to him a couple of times, but I haven't had time to go up myself.' He smiled slightly. 'I told him as much as I knew about her and he will be eager to talk to you.'

'I should hope so!' Her anger was now out in the open. She knew she should be grateful for his interest, but Aunt Betty was a special person and to have her shunted around between institutions without knowing about it, and without having any say, was really too much.

'I didn't intend to ignore you, Caro, but I didn't want you to be disappointed. It was quite possible that I was wrong.'

'And she would have been put back in the home, without my ever knowing she had been out of it?'

'No, of course not.' He sighed. This was becoming more difficult than he had thought it would be. It seemed the sparrow had a temper. He couldn't blame her, but he had forgotten about her aunt during the hectic last weeks. 'Can I drive you up to the station?'

'Yes, please.' As reluctant as she was to accept any further interventions from him at the moment, Caroline knew she would lose valuable time if she had to wait for a local bus. The only thing she could think of was to get to Aunt Betty as soon as possible. For some reason, nothing else seemed the least bit important. Something strange had happened to her aunt and Caroline had to be there. It felt as if her own life depended on it and she quickly started to get up, taking her mug into the kitchen.

'I'll phone Edward and say you are coming in.' David watched her quick movements and followed her smoothly.

'Yes, please. I think you should do that.' There was a thin veneer of ice in her voice and he sighed. It seemed as if he had miscalculated the degree of resentment his action might cause. He drove her to the station, accepting her cold withdrawal without comment.

Caroline's train journey seemed longer than usual and she prayed for no hold-ups on the Underground. She well remembered the route to the Heathfield and felt the old familiar feeling of welcome as she climbed the incline to the modern building. It was certainly different from the sprawling buildings of Castleview.

As she took the lift to the seventh floor and entered the psychiatric unit, she felt her anxiety rise. None of the staff was known to her and all of a sudden she was just a patient's visitor. She remembered the anxiety of relatives as they came to talk to the doctor and now she knew how they felt. The ward sister was new to her, but had obviously been expecting her.

'Oh, yes, hello, Miss Lawson. Dr Staveley knows you are coming. He says he will wait until you have had a visit with your aunt before meeting with you.' The cheerful face was smiling with understanding. 'I hear that you trained here?' She waited for Caroline's nod. 'Your aunt is in room sixteen, just down on the left. She's coming along very well and will just have finished lunch, I expect.'

Lunch? Aunt Betty? The nurses at the home had had to feed her. Caroline felt a surge of excitement. Could it be possible that her aunt might recover? She could feel her legs trembling as she walked down the familiar corridor and paused outside the half-open door. She knew it was a single room and she looked around the corner of the door before knocking. She saw the dear figure of Aunt Betty seated in a large easy chair, facing the window. Caroline felt a rush of affection. She hadn't seen her aunt sitting out of bed for over three years.

She knocked lightly. 'Aunt Betty? It's Caroline. I've come to see how you like it here.'

The pale face turned slightly and a small smile creased the deeply lined features. 'Hello, dear. It is nice of you to come.' Her voice was low and the words were spoken in a monotone, but Caroline felt tears of relief sting her eyes. These were the first words her aunt had said to her in years.

'Oh, Aunt Betty, I'm so glad to see you!' Caroline hurried over to the chair and bent to kiss the wrinkled cheek. She pulled up another chair and leaned over to hold the hands lying loosely over the warm blanket. Caroline could hardly believe what she was seeing. Her aunt recognised her and could speak. This seemed miraculous enough, but to understand that she was eating and talking to others seemed more than she could ever have hoped for.

In her relief, Caroline could hardly stop herself from talking. There was so much to say, so much time to fill in. She knew she was chattering and her words were tumbling over each other in her eagerness to share her new life at Castleview. The clouded brown eyes were watching her and the occasional smile crossed the elderly woman's features. Her hand softly stroked the young hands holding on to hers.

'I'm talking so much, you can't get a word in.' Caroline felt ashamed. She had so many questions, but didn't want to press her aunt.

'How is your young man?' The quiet eyes watched Caroline's face.

'Oh, you mean Dr Hunter. He's fine.' Caroline was not feeling very charitable towards this particular young man at the moment. 'He was the one who referred you here.'

Her aunt merely nodded and muttered lowly, 'A faithful friend is the medicine of life.'

Caroline again felt a rush of tenderness towards her aunt; even the old habit of quoting proverbs was coming back. It seemed a hint of the normality of their years spent together; perhaps the beginning of a return to health. As Caroline overcame her initial euphoria at the change in Aunt Betty, her clinical observation skills began to take over. She could see the elderly lady was still very ill and seemed distant from their conversation, as if she was preoccupied with other thoughts.

Caroline was reminded that she did not know the revised diagnosis for her aunt, or even if there was one. If there was no dementia, why was she so withdrawn and passive? It was time to talk with Dr Staveley. As Caroline bent to kiss her aunt goodbye she felt another wave of relief. At least she had Aunt Betty back. She promised to return to visit as soon as she could, and she made her way back to the sister's office to ask for an interview with the chief of the psychiatric unit.

Caroline entered Dr Staveley's office still filled with a sense of relief. Her aunt's progress did seem a miracle and, although she was still angry at David for not telling her what he had done, she would always have to be grateful to him.

'Hello, Caroline. Please sit down.' The tall, distinguished-looking man stood and moved around the front of his desk. 'I hope you will allow me to call you Caroline. I remember you from the time you spent on the unit here.'

'Of course, Dr Staveley.' She accepted the offered

chair and leaned forward. 'I want to thank you for all you have done for my aunt. She is so much improved, it's wonderful.'

The doctor slowly sat in a chair across from her. 'You have David Hunter to thank for that, I think. You know he referred her to me?'

Caroline nodded. She had not entirely made up her mind just how grateful she was for his actions.

'There is a good deal to tell you. Perhaps the best place to start is with our physical tests. All of our scans showed no evidence of any cortical atrophy and the neurologists could find no obvious abnormality.' He paused and smiled briefly. 'That left the field open for us. As I am sure you know, it is easy enough to miss psychological disturbance that can masquerade as organic disease. At any rate, we then started mild antidepressant medication.'

'EST?' Caroline interrupted. She knew that electro-shock therapy was occasionally used at Heathfield in cases of severe depression.

'No,' Dr Staveley shook his head, 'we needed her memory clear. There was no one who could tell us what might be troubling her. David said she had become ill when you started your nurses' training, so perhaps it was something to do with her feelings for you.'

'Me?'

'Perhaps she no longer felt as needed, once you had left home.' His hand lifted slightly off the arm of his chair.

'But that's not true!'

Edward Staveley again smiled quietly. 'Not from your point of view, but perhaps from hers. In any case, we needed her to be able to talk with us. And that we have achieved.' He paused and considered the young face across from him.

'She has talked to you?' Caroline's hopes rose. Aunt Betty might regain her health and be as she always was.

'Yes.' Again he paused. 'This is where the difficulties come in.' He watched her very carefully. 'I think you need to know more about your aunt. David has told me about your upbringing. . .'

Again, Caroline felt a stab of irritation. She didn't like to think of David discussing her behind her back. She kept silent, sensing the care the doctor was taking with his choice of words.

'In the first place, she is not your aunt. She is your mother.'

'Oh!' This revelation was not as much of a shock to Caroline as it might have been. She had always thought of Aunt Betty as her mother and had often wished she were. She smiled. 'I think that's lovely. I can't wait to tell her how much I have always wanted to call her "Mum".' She added more thoughtfully, 'Do you know who my father was?' She prayed silently that it wasn't her uncle.

'No, not precisely. Apparently she had an affair in her late thirties but she hasn't talked much about it. That doesn't seem to be a major contributing factor in her illness. She will undoubtedly be able to tell us that in due course. She certainly never regretted having you. You were the centre of her life.' He smiled warmly.

Caroline waited. She knew there must be more, but she was just relieved that she hadn't been her uncle's daughter.

'The cause of her guilt. . .' Edward Staveley was watching Caroline's face closely and seemed satisfied with her reaction to his information so far.

'Guilt?'

'Yes, your aunt—mother—is a very moral person, as I think you know. . .' Caroline nodded, as he continued '. . .and she performed an act for which she has never been able to forgive herself.' Again he paused.

Caroline kept her eyes fastened on the psychiatrist's face. What could meek and mild Aunt Betty—she couldn't yet call her mother—what could gentle Aunt Betty have ever done to cause herself such distress?

Dr Staveley's voice continued in a calm and professional tone. 'It seems she attacked her husband—your stepfather—and caused his back injury. Apparently she caused him to fall down the stairs and he spent the remainder of his life in a wheelchair.'

'Why?' Caroline could not remember ever seeing him out of the chair.

The doctor looked at her intently. 'This is where you come in, Caroline. Remember, you were the most important person in her world to her. You were her only child and she would have given her life for you. In a way, that is what she has done now.'

'Me?' Caroline could feel the familiar fluttering start inside her and she gripped the arms of her chair. She had a desire to run and concentrated every ounce of her will to sit and listen.

CHAPTER ELEVEN

DR STAVELEY leaned forward slightly, his calm dark eyes never leaving Caroline's face. 'She found your uncle attacking you. She heard you scream and rushed in to protect you. She says she hit him repeatedly—she doesn't remember how—and chased him away and he accidentally fell.' He paused before continuing quietly, 'She tended him the rest of his life, but made him live upstairs. You apparently lived in a room downstairs and she never let him be alone with you again, as long as he lived.' He sighed. 'That is her guilt, destroying a man's life—her husband's. To her that is an unforgivable sin and she has set her own penance. When she saw you safely into adulthood, she could withdraw into her pain.'

Caroline had closed her eyes and barely heard the last part of his gentle words. She could remember, distantly, noise and pain and fear, but there were no visual images, just sound and feelings. She could feel herself start to shake and she hugged herself tightly.

'Caroline. . .' The quiet voice cut through her confused thoughts. 'Caroline, it is unlikely you would remember. You were very small. Do you remember anything?'

She shook her head slowly, still clinging in her own arms. 'No, not really. . .just horrible feelings.' She opened her eyes to look at the understanding face watching her.

He nodded. 'Yes, you must have been terrified, without knowing why. Now you know why. . .' He leaned forward slightly. 'Have the feelings lasted?'

'Yes. Yes, they have.' She loosened her arms slightly. Suddenly she felt very tired. 'Whenever there is a threat of violence. Even if it isn't actual, just if I think there might be. And. . .' she paused and looked at the knowledgeable psychiatrist '. . .and probably. . .sex.' She couldn't really tell him anything more.

He nodded silently. There was something she needed to know. She swallowed; her mouth felt very dry. She took a deep breath and let her arms fall to the edge of the chair. 'Did he. . .was he. . .abusing me?'

Dr Staveley looked at her quietly. 'That we will never know. Your aunt doesn't know. She just saw you in danger and acted with the strength of rage.' He smiled at her softly. 'The exact nature of an attack is not so important to a child as it is to an adult. To a child, pain is fearful and a horror regardless of the cause. You were being hurt and were screaming with fear. That your mother knows for a certainty. That is all we know.'

Caroline sat in silence, thinking of the past. So many small details were beginning to make sense—her seemingly unfounded dislike of her uncle, Aunt Betty's watchfulness, even why she had had her own special room behind the kitchen downstairs that had always been her private refuge. She breathed deeply and looked up at the doctor.

'All those years. . .she protected me.'

He nodded without speaking.

'Will she get better, do you think?'

'It will take time. She needs to forgive herself.' He leaned back, now thinking of his patient. 'She had to make a choice, between husband and child. She has yet to understand or accept that a mother has no choice. The child must always be protected. That is a biological truth we ignore at our peril.' He smiled to himself and glanced at Caroline. 'You must excuse me. I tend to turn into a scientist too easily.'

Caroline nodded. She didn't know what she would have done in the same situation. 'Can I help her? By talking about this. . .?' She recognised the depth of her debt to her mother.

'Perhaps.' The psychiatrist moved back slightly in his chair. 'That will come later, when she has a greater awareness of how others can forgive. At the moment she is still blaming herself.' He looked at Caroline with a quiet calmness. 'Is there anything you would like to talk about, now, with me?'

'I don't think so. At least, not right now. I need time to think. . .' She was grateful to this skilled doctor, but there was too much information to digest before she could talk rationally about her feelings.

'Well, should you ever wish to, my door is open. . .' He turned slightly and pushed a button on his intercom. 'I have asked David to come and drive you home. I hope you don't mind, but I did not wish you to leave here alone.'

Caroline bristled slightly, but she was really feeling too tired to argue. Suddenly she remembered Aunt Betty's—no, her mother's—words. 'A faithful friend is the medicine of life.' She smiled wryly. Perhaps she was right. The sight of the orange Mini did nothing to soften Caroline's feelings towards David. She supposed she should be grateful he hadn't brought the battered van, and climbed in with a brief acknowledgement to him.

'Care to stop for a coffee?' David kept his voice carefully neutral. He had had a long talk with Edward Staveley and knew the content of Caroline's interview. He had not been particularly surprised as he had guessed that Caroline's 'flutterings' might have been based on a childhood fear. He knew his reaction would have to be carefully controlled. She wasn't going to like his knowing anything she hadn't told him herself.

'No, thank you. I think I would just like to go back.' Caroline watched the early evening twilight settle over the city as they wove their way through the rush-hour traffic. Her mind was busy with a multitude of thoughts and they drove in silence.

By the time they reached Castleview it was dark and

David watched her enter the residence. His heart ached for the solitude he knew she was experiencing. Still, he had work to do. As he shifted gears he could feel the unaccustomed weight in the car. Ten litres of paint and a few other parcels could weigh a fair amount, and he looked forward to getting to work on producing the mushroom-coloured walls favoured by a very special young woman.

The trip up to London had been useful and he contentedly unloaded the variety of containers he had collected. Another late night lay ahead, but this he would enjoy. For some reason he felt a sense of urgency to make his tiny new home habitable.

Caroline also spent a largely sleepless night. Her thoughts were whirling in uncontrollable patterns of confused memories. She tossed, trying to find a comfortable spot in bed, but she couldn't settle and finally gave up. She sat up and put on the low bedside lamp. Her mind was too busy to allow her to read, but perhaps if she wrote down her thoughts she might be able to make some order out of what Dr Staveley had told her.

The night seemed quiet and peaceful and she remembered how much she had enjoyed doing night duty. Nights on a psychiatric ward might be very interesting, she thought. If she couldn't sleep, how must the seriously disturbed get through the black hours?

She wrote slowly and carefully, trying to put her thoughts in order. As her eyelids were beginning to feel heavy, she looked at her illuminated clock. Four o'clock. These were always the dead hours, between four and five. The last period of quiet before the beginning of the work for the six o'clock chores on the ward.

A series of soft thuds caught her attention. If she hadn't been awake, she wouldn't have heard them. Who could be creeping around at this ungodly hour?

Feeling distinctly nervous, Caroline unbolted her door and peered down the dark corridor. There were pale night lights in the hall but they didn't allow a very clear view of the shadowed hallway. She put on her slippers and robe, and opened her door a bit further.

She took a deep breath and reminded herself that if she could deal with Martin's behaviour, she could confront an intruder. She looked around for a weapon. All she could think of was a long rolled-up umbrella, and she clutched it purposefully.

'Who's there?' she called with all the authority she could muster, and ventured one step out into the corridor.

At the sound of her voice a definite thud was heard at the opposite end of the hall as a heavy object landed on the floor. It was the residence thief! Caroline felt her blood boil.

'You put that down!' Her voice was loud and clear. She didn't know exactly what she meant. He had probably already dropped whatever he was carrying, but she suddenly felt a surge of anger. People had no right to steal from other people! 'Just what do you think you are doing?'

This time her voice was close to screeching level, and she could hear a tinge of hysteria in her own ears. For some reason, it felt good to yell. She took a deep breath and bellowed down the hall. 'Don't you *dare! Don't you dare!*'

She heard doors opening and suddenly a robed figure shot past her and ran down to the end of the corridor. She heard a shout, a loud scuffle, and a sharp crack as if a solid object had hit the floor.

'Got him!' It was Andrew's voice and he sounded triumphant.

At the head of the stairs, Andrew was sitting on what looked like a heap of grey rags. The grey heap was making muffled groaning sounds. Andrew gave it a thump. 'Belt up. I'm not moving, so you can just put a lid on it.'

He looked up and grinned happily at Caroline. 'You certainly can make a fine noise, woman. Look what we've found.' He shifted slightly, keeping his weight firmly balanced on the heap.

Caroline bent over to look at the face under the grey overcoat. She had never seen it before. 'Who's he?'

'He's our Castleview creeper, that's who he is. None

other than good old Charlie!' Andrew was positively gleeful.

'Charlie? The porter?' Caroline was astonished. 'Why on earth would he want to steal things?' She suddenly grasped her umbrella more firmly. This was the evil person who had framed Terry.

'Probably in hock to a few bookies. But we've got him. Could someone please call the authorities? I'm getting tired of sitting on this dirty old muckheap.'

It was another hour before they had finished with the hospital security people, and Charlie had been removed by the local police.

Caroline was exhausted and flopped into her bed. Charlie had admitted to putting Fred's watch into the workbench drawer when he had been interrupted during a search for portable power tools, hoping to divert suspicion. As she was trying to think of a way Terry could be told that the real thief had been found, her mind finally succumbed to an overwhelming need for sleep.

She awoke again to the shaft of sunlight poking its bright fingers around the edges of her curtain. She groaned and tried to shield her eyes by rolling over. It was no use. She sat up slowly and looked at her clock. Seven. She had had all of two hours' sleep. Well, she had survived on less than that before now. Before staggering to the bath, she looked at the papers scattered over her desk. It was too soon to look at what she had written during the night.

Feeling slightly more awake after a brisk scrub, she peeked cautiously at the outside world. It looked like the beginning of a beautiful day and she squinted against the light. She had a sudden urge to go into the village. It was Sunday; she could go to the church and if she saw the vicar she would tell him about Charlie.

Her spirits lightened as she tiptoed out of the residence. The morning light was pale, giving a shimmering edge to the bare branches of the trees overhead. The road to the village was deserted and the peaceful silence had a calm stillness. Caroline could feel her tired body relaxing as she pedalled evenly and breathed in the clean air.

At the church she saw the vicar's battered automobile still parked outside. The service had not yet finished and she slipped in quietly. The closing prayers were being said and she added a few short words of her own, before the small congregation began to leave.

Again the vicar recognised her and accepted her news with a slight, sad shake of his head. He had no further information about Terry and she slowly wheeled her bicycle back through the village.

She stopped outside the chemist's shop and looked up at the first floor. Those windows were still clouded with dust. She shook her head slowly. On such a sunlit day they should sparkle. Those window-ledges looked wide enough to hold flower-boxes, she thought, as she visualised a generous overflow of summer blossoms. Perhaps the odd red geranium might look pretty.

On an impulse she gave the doorbell a quick push. She shouldn't disturb him, but at least she could offer to wash the windows. The raising of a sash window made her look up to see the head and broad shoulders of David leaning out.

'Hello?' He sounded slightly groggy and Caroline felt a slight tug at her heart.

'Hello. I'm sorry. Did I get you up?' She was slightly embarrassed. He had probably been sleeping late to catch up on all his missed nights.

'That's OK.' He disappeared with an indistinct mumble that Caroline didn't quite hear. She thought she could pick out the words 'sparrows' and 'early birds' but she wasn't sure. The door buzzer sounded and she hauled the bicycle into the narrow hallway. Climbing the stairs, she found the door to the flat open and a strong odour of fresh paint wafting down.

'You've been painting already?' She walked into the small sitting-room and looked around at the walls. They were spotless, covered with an even coat of light beige paint. Her eyes were caught by the addition of some very colourful large cushions on the floor. They looked like the bean bags children used for bouncing in.

David came in, carrying two mugs of tea. 'This time we have milk.' He motioned her to one of the cushions. 'Courtesy of the local Women's Institute. They came from the community centre, used in the village nursery, I think.' He sat down gingerly after handing her a mug. 'I'll give them back when I get some furniture, but they're really very comfy.'

As she sat down, Caroline felt herself engulfed in the squishy pillow. She spilled a little of the tea as she found her knees rapidly approaching her chin. 'Oh. . .'

'Not to worry. They wash. They will also get new covers, if they're here for any length of time.' He eyed the flowered chintz with slightly bleary eyes.

'Were you still asleep? I'm sorry. . .' Caroline felt guilty; he did look exhausted.

'Not still. Haven't been to bed yet.' He waved a hand at the walls. 'I wanted to get it done.'

'They look lovely. Really they do.' The improvement was obvious and already the room was getting a home-like air. She could feel her tired bones sinking into the thick cushion and stirred herself. She didn't want to fall asleep here. 'I wanted to tell you we caught the thief last night.'

David listened to her story with interest and grinned at her version of Andrew sitting triumphantly on Charlie's collapsed person. 'And you were the one who woke everybody up?'

Caroline nodded. 'I just yelled.' She smiled at the memory. 'I felt like screaming, and I must admit it felt good to screech at the top of my lungs.'

David smiled quietly and nodded. 'I should imagine it did.' As he carefully set his mug on the floor he said, 'That means you haven't had much sleep.'

She shook her head. 'No. I wanted to write down. . .things. . .' She wasn't sure how much she wanted to tell him, at least right now. 'Before I could get to bed, Charlie arrived on the scene and then the security lot and the police. . .' She could feel herself wanting to yawn and she swallowed. She was really feeling very tired indeed. All that cycling had probably been a silly idea.

David extricated himself from his bean bag with difficulty. 'You can bunk down here. The camp-bed is reasonably comfortable.'

'Oh, no, I couldn't do that.' Caroline felt she should object for some reason, but her bones were complaining loudly at the thought of riding back to residence.

'Better that than falling off the Blue Bomber, and I'm not up to driving you back—I'd doze off at the wheel.' He shuffled out of the room and could be heard moving around, making various thumping sounds in one of the bedrooms.

Caroline tried to shift herself and found she couldn't get up out of the bag. It seemed to have her in its clutches and she muttered darkly.

'Alley-oop!' With a quick movement, David lifted her out with a swoop of his arms and she found herself being held lightly against a warm chest. She could feel the smooth muscles against her and his breath was warm and soft against her cheek. 'Come on, sleepy head.' He gently kissed the top of her nose and purposefully steered her towards the back bedroom. 'Your cosy bed awaits.'

Caroline looked at the narrow bed that looked so inviting, with clean sheets and fluffy pillow under a blue blanket. She wondered sleepily if he chose blue especially. Her brain was too tired to think about it.

'You'll find a bathrobe on the door if you want it. Sleep tight.' With a soft kiss on her cheek, he left her, quietly shutting the door behind him. All Caroline could think of was climbing between those lovely clean, cool sheets and she quickly undressed and crawled in. The bed was very narrow, but she really didn't care and stretched out to wait for sleep.

As her body relaxed, her mind kept whirling. Thoughts of strange scary noises in the night, a woman's face that changed from Aunt Betty's to an unknown old woman crying, a jumble of sensations of new paint spiced with the smell of pine, and soft pillows that felt strong and safe—all combined to keep her restless and wide awake. She turned over on her back and stared up at the ceiling. There was a long crooked crack in one corner.

When she squinted at it with her head tilted, it looked like a craggy mountain.

Giving up on sleep, Caroline decided to try a hot bath. She might even have to resort to hot milk, now that he had some. Pulling on the robe from the back of the door, she padded into the bathroom. Since he didn't seem to have any bath oils or bubbly things, Caroline settled for a plain hot soak.

She let her limbs float in the heat and idly dribbled drops of water on her stomach. Her sleepy mind drifted off in the steamy haze. She peered down at her body. It wasn't so bad, was it? All pink and shiny. Looked a bit like a cooked lobster. She giggled softly.

You know what you want, woman. You want to climb mountains—with a particular mountain climber. One who has sunlit hair and smooth skin and smells of fresh air. She felt deliciously soft and supple as she climbed out of the heat and dried off with a lovely fluffy towel; this time green, she noted. She pulled on the robe and walked determinedly to the door of David's bedroom.

Opening the door quietly, she peeked in. He was fast asleep, wrapped up in what looked like two sleeping-bags on the floor. She could see his strong profile in the pale sunlight coming through the uncurtained window. He looked so young and vulnerable and she crept closer to watch him breathing. He was wearing crumpled pyjamas and one arm was flung out of the cover. He was lying in an open sprawl flat on his back, with the edge of the zippered bag tucked around his hips.

Caroline looked at that zipper with a cautious eye. She wondered how one managed this sort of thing without getting sliced by incautious moves. Well, she decided, David would know. He probably managed very well. If she didn't hurry up, she would change her mind. She poked him tentatively in the arm.

'Wha. . .?' He mumbled and turned over, continuing to breathe deeply.

Caroline poked him again, this time a little harder, in the back. He didn't seem to feel it and, just as she was preparing to try again, he suddenly sharply turned back to her.

'What is it, Caro? What's wrong?' His eyes were wide open and he was looking at her searchingly. Years of waking up suddenly in the middle of the night had produced an instant result. Caroline gulped.

'N. . .nothing. Nothing's wrong. . .' She stammered slightly. 'At least. . .'

He shook his head slowly and sank back down on the sleeping-bag. He looked up at her. 'Hmm? Then what is it?'

Caroline took a deep breath and spoke very clearly. 'I would like. . .please. . . David, would you please make love to me?' There. She had said it.

'Will it. . .? Will I. . .what?' He peered at her with a puzzled look.

'I said——' Caroline spoke a little less loudly.

He brushed his hands over his eyes. 'I heard what you said. I just didn't believe it.' He moaned slightly. 'Do you know what time it is?'

Caroline felt slightly confused. 'I don't know. About twelve, I guess. Why?'

David mumbled sleepily, 'High noon. How appropriate.' He rolled over to take a closer look at her. She was perched beside him on the floor wearing a too-large bathrobe and nothing else, as far as he could see. 'I don't suppose you'd care to tell me what this is all about?'

Caroline frowned slightly. This wasn't going as she had planned. Well, she hadn't exactly planned anything. But she had thought everything just. . .happened. He wasn't reacting as she had thought he would. 'I don't know. . .does it have to be about anything?'

He squinted at her and rubbed his face with a large hand. 'Well, yes, Caro. It's usually about something.' He sighed and propped his head up on one hand to watch her face. 'About a lot of different things. I'm just wondering which one you had in mind.'

Caroline hadn't expected a cross-examination and she was beginning to regret her impulse. He just didn't want her and she was silly to think that he might have. She lowered her head and looked at her hands clutching the bathrobe. It didn't even have any ties. Stupid bathrobe.

David looked at the downcast face and sighed. Slowly

he disentangled himself from the sleeping-bag and crawled out.

'Where are you going?' Her voice was very small. Now he was going away to leave her alone.

He looked down at her with a serious expression. 'In case you didn't know it, Caro, there are certain requirements for gentlemen about to perform a service for a lady.' He stretched slowly. 'They have to be awake, for one thing. I am going to try and wake up.' With that firm statement he disappeared in the direction of the bathroom and she heard the sound of the shower from behind the door.

She sat quietly, thinking. He did seem very serious about it all. She didn't want him to feel obligated. And maybe he'd be disappointed. After she'd woken him up, when she really shouldn't have. . .

By the time he returned, smelling of fresh soap, she was beginning to have deep doubts as to the wisdom of her actions.

David looked down at the slim figure sitting on the floor. Those enormous brown eyes were full of sleep and confusion. He sat down slowly, and gently took one of the tightly clasped hands. 'Now, Caro, I am awake, or as awake as I can get.' He patted the hand he held. 'What brought you in here?'

Caroline tried to think. 'I couldn't sleep. The bed was too narrow.'

David hid a smile. 'I see. You are welcome to a sleeping-bag.'

She could feel her irritation rising. He was being deliberately obtuse. 'I don't want a sleeping-bag. I want. . .' She stopped.

He said quietly, 'You are telling me you want sex.'

She nodded, mutely. It didn't sound the least bit romantic when he said it that way.

'Why me?' His question sounded conversational.

She looked at him wide-eyed. 'Who else is there? I don't know anybody else.' She heard herself with a start of surprise. That wasn't what she had meant to say at all.

David placed her captive hand on his chest and she

could feel his heart beating under her palm, 'Feel this, Caro?' She nodded. 'Well, that is a heart that belongs to you. It always will.' He removed her hand and gently brushed it with his lips. 'For better or worse, as they say.'

She could feel tears sting her eyes. He was saying he loved her! This wonderful man, who could have any woman in the world, was saying he loved *her*. She wanted to fling her arms around his neck, but there was something about the way he was looking at her that held her back.

'What I want to know, my love, is—what you think you want from me now.'

'I just. . .' She couldn't explain—that she wanted to be a part of him, to have him be a part of her. 'I thought you would know what to do!' she burst out.

He raised his eyebrows and watched her quizzically. 'And I am an expert, you think?'

She nodded.

He sighed heavily. 'I assume I am expected to take that as a compliment.' He turned her hand over thoughtfully. 'And upon what evidence do you base this idea?'

'Henry.' Her voice was barely above a whisper.

'Ah, so.' He looked up with a brightness in his eyes. 'Now we get to it. Henry, is it? Well, perhaps I should tell you about the lady Henrietta.'

Caroline wasn't sure she wanted to hear about this person, certainly not right now. She pulled her hand away and he let it go.

David sat back on his heels, regarding her silently, and then sat cross-legged on top of the bag. He patted the part beside him. 'Sit.' Caroline looked at him suspiciously. What was he up to now? But the floor was cold so she shuffled across to the soft quilted bag.

'Good.' He watched her reluctant move quietly. 'Now, remember the patient in London?' Caroline nodded. 'Well, that patient was, and is, Henry.' She stared at him. 'Yes, the lady Henrietta is a very troubled young woman. She gets herself into all sorts of difficulties and I was supposed to try and prevent some of those difficulties.' He looked down at his hands. 'I didn't do very well, I'm afraid.' At any rate, she is now in a London clinic and getting the treatment she probably should have had years ago.' He looked sideways at her. 'And I was paid, very well paid, to chaperon the lady Henry.'

Caroline looked at him, appalled. What did he mean? She thought there were words for such men, but she couldn't think of what they were.

David read the expression on her face very accurately and took a deep breath. How could this innocent know what he was talking about? 'Her father provided a scholarship that I won, early on at medical school. I met him through that and felt I owed him a debt. As I was studying psychiatry, he asked for my help with his daughter.' He added, without looking at her, 'I also needed the extra income. It was convenient to Castleview and my duties were not onerous.' He turned to look at her intently. 'I was not sleeping with the lady, Caro. She had plenty of other resources for that activity.' He turned back to look at the floor. 'Too many, I'm afraid.'

He uncrossed his legs. 'Anyway, that is the saga of the lady known as Henry. Even the rich can get sick, my love.'

Caroline tried to make sense of what she had heard. She knew Henry had seemed rather flighty and odd, but she hadn't seen her as a psychiatric patient. Somehow it was hard to imagine people outside the hospital as being ill, but then they must be at times; it wasn't only coming into hospital that meant someone needed professional help.

As she was puzzling over this thought, she was startled by David's hands under her hips, moving her off the top of the sleeping-bag.

'And now, I think we should get on with the service you need, my love.' He was straightening out the bag and carefully placing the zipper under the folds, she noticed.

She watched him with some nervousness. She wasn't so sure that she wanted him to do anything. She was beginning to feel drained and empty, and was not really thinking too clearly at all.

'Lie down.' His voice was quiet and authoritative.

Caroline looked at him with wide eyes. Well, she had started this, she supposed she had to go through with it. She backed down on her elbows, still watching him.

David kept his face in a serious expression. 'No. Roll over, on your tummy.'

Roll over? What on earth was he going to do? Caroline frowned at him.

David just looked at her. 'Whose bedroom are you in?'

'Yours.' Her voice was very low.

'So who's in charge here?'

'You.' There was a tiny choking sound as she answered.

'So do as I say. On your tum, please.'

Caroline slowly rolled over and heard him rustling behind her back and felt a soft, rolled-up jumper being placed under her head and shoulders.

'Now, put your arms up. . .no, wait just a minute.' Caroline felt him removing her robe and she shivered. 'There, that's better. Arms over the pillow. . .there. No, head to the side, please.' She felt her head being turned and she had to admit she did feel very comfortable. His jumper smelled faintly of pine-scented aftershave, and she closed her eyes.

David settled himself beside her and looked softly at the slim, exposed back. 'Have to feed up this sparrow,' he muttered as he lightly placed his hands on either side of the slender neck arched over the pillow. His hands slowly stroked the glowing skin under his palms. He stopped briefly to pull up the coverings over the smoothly rounded hips and tucked them in closely. 'Mustn't catch cold.'

He continued to murmur soft words as his large hands stroked and kneaded her neck and shoulders. He felt the muscles loosening and he gradually moved his hands lower down her back, continuing with an even pressure to ease the tension at each vertebra.

Caroline had a sleepy thought. For a doctor, he does give very good back-rubs. That's supposed to be a nursing skill. She was feeling deliciously relaxed—floating again.

She turned her head slightly to look at him. 'David?'

'Hmm?' He could hear the sleepiness in her voice and sighed. If she didn't go off soon, he was going to fall asleep himself.

'Can we climb mountains some day?' Her words were indistinct.

'Yes, my love. We will climb mountains.' His hands kept up their steady rhythm.

'You'll teach me how to climb?' She was barely awake, beginning to dream of tall pine trees encircling snow-capped mountains.

'Yes, Caro, I'll teach you to climb.' David stifled a yawn. But not right now, my love, I haven't got the energy.

He felt her sink down into the quilting and he maintained his soft massage until he heard her quiet, even breathing. Thank heaven, he thought, and lowered himself down beside her. He tucked the dark head under his shoulder, pulled up the warm covering over them both and heaved a deep sigh. A near thing there, old man. Thought you'd never get any sleep today.

When she awoke, Caroline squinted at the bare window. It was a second before she remembered where she was and she looked beside her. The sleeping-bag was empty and felt cold to her cautiously searching hand. She sat up. She was absolutely naked. Just like that Henry, she thought, and then she remembered. Everything he had said. Everything he had done. Or not done. She reached for the robe and clutched it around her.

She was ravenously hungry and remembered she had had only a cup of tea all day. She could hear noises in the kitchen and darted into the back room to find her clothing. By the time she was dressed, she could smell some very appetising food and she entered the kitchen slowly.

'Good afternoon.' David was busily stirring a large saucepan. 'Hunter's stew coming up.' He looked as refreshed as if he had had a week's sleep instead of probably about four or five hours. Caroline watched him carefully. She didn't know what to say about their sleeping arrangements.

He grinned at her. 'Sit yourself down. Soup spoons in the drawer behind you.' He brought over the saucepan and began to ladle out a portion of thick stew. 'I forgot to get bread, but this should at least keep us alive.'

Caroline started to eat and could feel the welcome arrival of food in a very empty stomach. She sighed with satisfaction and watched him as he ate. They were back in a kitchen again, sitting across a table. But this is better, she thought. This is a real kitchen—a home kitchen. She glanced up at the walls as she stirred her stew. Yes, yellow would be perfect.

'This is good.' She smiled at him. Did he expect her to say anything about last night? Or this morning, or whatever it was. The days and nights had become all mixed up.

He nodded. 'Needs more pepper, though.' He didn't move and Caroline smiled to herself. At least he didn't seem too fussy an eater. Why should you care? she said silently to herself. You're not doing the cooking. But you'd like to, answered another voice in her head.

She tried to think of something to distract her from such thoughts of domesticity, but before she came up with anything the door buzzer sounded in a long ring.

'Probably my landlord, asking for professional guidance.' David put his empty bowl in the sink and left to go down to the door at the bottom of the stairs.

Caroline took her own bowl to the sink and was washing them when he came back. Without turning, she said, 'Do you think we could let Terry know about catching Charlie?'

Not hearing an answer, she turned to see David standing inside the door with a strained expression on his face. He looked terribly tired again. 'I wondered——'

'No, Caro,' he looked up at her, 'I'm afraid we can't tell Terry. He died three hours ago.'

CHAPTER TWELVE

CAROLINE cycled slowly back to the residence through the pale twilight. David had gone over to speak with Mr Mapley and would return to the hospital to start on the paperwork connected with the sad news.

There was a numbness inside her that prevented her from feeling anything about Terry or David or herself. It all seemed much too complicated. She slept deeply and dreamlessly and woke to start a month of day duty with a strange feeling that perhaps the last four weeks really hadn't happened at all.

She noticed the staff looked as usual during the weekend report from the night staff. Meg was as brisk as always, and Caroline made her morning round of the ward and helped at breakfast. She saw that Mr Vanijek was absent and, although she looked for him, he was not on the ward. She reported his absence calmly to Meg, who simply noted the time of her report and nodded. Somehow Caroline found she couldn't even react to this patient's unexpected departure.

She helped the patients make their beds and again accompanied Mr Lawrence over to OT, where she found her still unfinished footstool under the worktable. As she started to work on the plastic strips she glanced over at Terry's corner. Eric was helping another patient set up a work project. He wasn't a Folkestone patient, and she looked around at the others. Bob was still thumping nails into some wood, Fred was energetically punching holes into a leather belt and Mr Lawrence was starting another footstool.

Nothing seemed to have changed. Caroline sighed. She wondered what the patients were thinking. In the morning meeting, David had quietly announced that Terry would not be coming back, and if they wished they could discuss the matter later in their individual groups. He had said that Terry had died in hospital after

contracting a blood infection and the funeral would be
on Wednesday in the local church. No more had been
said. Caroline suspected that the patients had already
known of Terry's death—such information could never
be kept from the efficient hospital grapevine. No one
had asked any questions and the usual silence had
descended on the group until Bob had excused himself,
again as he always did.

There were some newly admitted patients on the ward
and the usual routines continued. It was decided in a
staff meeting that Winston would remain on the ward on
Wednesday afternoon to enable as many staff as wished
to attend the village service. Otherwise, there was no
discussion of Terry; there seemed to be enough work to
keep all staff occupied. Everyone knew that the porter
had been the cause of the thefts but no mention was
made of this. Fred seemed quieter than usual and had
made no complaints in the meeting.

Her return to day duty meant that she could not play
the piano in the evenings for the group, so Caroline did
not know what was happening with the singing group.
She assumed they would continue if they wished,
although Mr Vanijek's disappearance meant there was
no one to play for them. She had seen David only in
passing as they were both busy. He had always smiled at
her, but seemed to be moving at his usual hectic pace
around the hospital.

Caroline finished her shift early on Wednesday and
hurried to change, choosing to wear a dark brown jacket
over her light brown woollen skirt, with her usual white
blouse. The day was balmy and she realised it was the
first day of March. It seemed unfair to Terry to have his
funeral on one of the first days of a real spring.

As she was unlocking the bicycle, wondering how her
skirt would fare on the ride to the village, she gratefully
smiled at Andrew's quiet voice.

'I'm going in to the church, Caroline. Want to ride in
questionable comfort?' His friendly face looked solemn
as he motioned towards the front door.

'Have you got yourself transport, then, Andrew?' She

was pleased to have a faster way of reaching the village. She didn't want to be late on this special day.

'Only an old banger.' He was leading the way around the residence and stopped beside a small car. 'Second-hand from a departing staff nurse.' As they settled themselves, he continued, 'It seems I'll be here for a while, so the investment was sensible. It makes travelling easier.'

Caroline didn't know who else would be at the service, and she was pleased to find the church filled to capacity. She had expected to see the local people attend, but was surprised to see a number of Castleview staff, standing at the sides. She noticed Eric standing under one of the windows and looked around to see if any of the Folkestone patients had come. For a moment she couldn't see any of them, and then she saw that the front rows on the left were filled with familiar heads. They were all seated together and she guessed they had come in hospital transport.

She stood at the back as the vicar began the service, her eyes straying to the casket at the front of the chapel. It was covered with mauve and white flowers, and with a tiny wrench of pain she recognised Mrs Wenham's crocuses. There were small bouquets of the same blooms placed on small pedestals on either side; the effect was simple and delicate.

The vicar spoke quietly, talking about Terry, and then he started a hymn. As Caroline joined in with the familiar words, she strained to see the small organ, but her view was blocked.

As the main congregation sat down, the vicar looked down at them. 'This is the time when I would normally ask others to speak about Terry, and I know there are many of you here who knew him well.' He paused. 'Terry's family has requested that we do not follow the formal service today, but allow others to participate in any way they feel is appropriate.'

He turned slightly to his right and nodded briefly before turning back to the congregation. 'A friend of Terry's has requested that he be allowed to pay a tribute.'

He looked out over the heads of the patients and smiled quietly. 'It is a pleasure to introduce Mr Anton Vanijek.'

Caroline felt her heart thud as the silver-grey head of the musician became visible. Anton Vanijek was wearing full formal evening dress and in his hand he carried a gleaming violin. Caroline's eyes widened in surprise. This was not Eric's violin. This was the Maestro's famous Guarnieri, and the instrument glowed with burnished light. So this was where he had gone—home to get his own violin.

Caroline glanced over at Eric. The craftsman's eyes were fastened on the musician and his face lit up with respect and pride. This was what he had hoped for, thought Caroline—to see and hear his countryman play again. It seemed as if Eric were standing to attention as his eyes never wavered from the slightly stooped figure that was standing motionless, with bowed head, before the flower-draped casket.

Then, with slow deliberate movements, Anton Vanijek raised the violin to his shoulder and bent his head as if to caress it. He raised the bow and slowly drew it across the strings and a sweet searing note trembled in the expectant silence.

Caroline could feel her eyes sting. She knew what he was going to play, and she could feel the loosening of the grief she had been holding in so tightly. As the familiar phrases of Schubert's *Ave Maria* floated over their heads, she watched the great musician play with all the intensity, concentration and power of genius. He had regained his self, the inner being that belonged to music. He and his instrument were again one and this patient had become whole again.

As the poignant prayer soared through the arched ceiling and out into the spring air, she felt a lightening of her sorrow, as if the music were releasing her to again hope and believe in life. A patient had come to life again and was honouring his young friend with the greatest gift he could give—himself.

As the music drifted away into silence, Anton Vanijek bowed slightly in the direction of the casket and lifted his head to speak to the silent congregation.

'We would now like to offer a tribute from the Castleview choir under the direction of Miss Caroline Lawson.' He caught Caroline's eyes as she looked at him in amazement. What did he mean? She looked at him with wide eyes and he simply inclined his head towards the group seated in the front rows.

Caroline moved forward slowly. She knew she had no choice, and as she did so she saw Mr Vanijek quietly walk over to the organ. He placed his violin in a case on the floor, closed it and took his place at the tiny instrument.

As she reached the front of the church, she looked over at the front rows. She saw her singing group, carefully seated according to their groups for the Mozart, and they were all watching her solemnly. Well, if that was what they intended, so be it. She paused briefly as she passed the casket, and looked at the flowers. They were really very beautiful and she knew Terry would have liked them.

She stood silently in front of the group and slowly let her gaze move over them. Gladys was seated in front of Bob, Mr Lawrence was at the back, and she was slightly surprised to see David sitting in a back row beside Martin, holding a sheet of music. So he intended to sing. Nothing should really surprise her about these people. All right, then, she thought. If it's the Mozart, we might as well get on with it.

She slowly raised her hands and the group rose as a single person. Everyone was watching her with undivided concentration and she nodded to Mr Vanijek. As the soft chords began, she cued the group and heard the expected even unison. They were singing with serious intent and controlled energy. There were no dangling voices, no hanging notes. Their music was strong and steady, building a crescendo of magnificent sound that filled the church.

Not once did a single voice waver. She could hear David's strong tenor holding the men on the melody, and Gladys was singing her light soprano line with sureness and clarity. They responded to every flick of her fingertips with certainty, ending quietly in clean unison. After the final soft organ notes faded, she slowly lowered her hands and they sat down with a single movement.

Caroline smiled softly at them and nodded to Mr Vanijek before walking back down the aisle to take her place at the rear of the church. So that is what it's all about, she thought. When they need you, you go. When they no longer need you, you leave. Her heart was lighter as she waited for the vicar to complete the service. Her people had said goodbye to Terry in their own way and she had helped them to do it.

She stood aside as the procession led the way out of the church, and she looked for David. She noticed him shepherding the Folkestone group down towards a side door. By the time she managed to leave behind the others, she could see the hospital van was ready to leave. She waved and saw a few nodding heads through the windscreen.

A light tap on her shoulder caused her to turn, to see Anton Vanijek with a coat covering his formal attire and his violin case tucked securely under his arm.

'I wish to say goodbye, Miss Lawson. It has been a pleasure.' He gave his courtly little bow and Caroline shook his offered hand.

'Are you going home, then, Mr Vanijek? I wish you well.' How simple the words sounded, she thought. Yet that was exactly what she did wish, for all of them.

He nodded. 'Thank you. It is time to return, I think. Yes, it is time.'

She couldn't help herself asking, 'Will you play again, do you think? In public?'

The slightly hunched shoulders shrugged slightly. 'That I do not know. Perhaps. I will have much relearning to do.' He gave a little smile. 'I am old now to work so hard, but perhaps. . .'

'I hope so, Mr Vanijek. I really hope you do. But most of all, be well.' She grasped his hand tightly. This was how she would like to say farewell to all of the patients. She watched him walk away from the crowd towards a large black car waiting for him. As she continued to watch, she saw a uniformed driver quickly open the rear

passenger door and Mr Vanijek disappeared from view.
It seemed his world had reclaimed him and she could
only hope that it treated him gently.

Caroline turned to follow the villagers to the churchyard. She wanted to see Terry laid to rest; it was a
necessary part of the leave-taking. He would be back in
his home, in safety and peace.

She saw a fair head towering above the gathered
mourners and she went to stand behind that broad
shoulder. It felt the right place for her to be and she
stood silently. David turned slightly, as if aware of her
unspoken presence, and took her hand, drawing her
close to his side.

They stood and watched as the casket was lowered.
The flowers had been removed and Caroline could see
they were all groups of bulbs in small pots. As the vicar
spoke the final words and the crowd murmured its
goodbyes, Mrs Wenham began to pick up some of the
flowering crocuses and packed them into small boxes.
She noticed Caroline watching and brought over a small
pot.

'Would you like one, dear? We give them to the older
parishioners and they keep very well. I do this every
spring and I thought Terry would have liked them, as
well.'

'They looked beautiful, Mrs Wenham. Thank you.'
Caroline looked at the white and mauve flowers. 'You
were right. They are a sign of hope.' She smiled at the
nodding woman who began to energetically pack her
blooms into the battered estate wagon.

'So life goes on,' Caroline murmured, touching the
delicate oval-shaped petals.

'Yes, it does. Where do you want to put those?' David
squeezed her hand lightly.

'I don't know.' She held the pot carefully. The vicar
had gone over to talk to a group of villagers which
included the Mapley family. 'Should we go over there?'

'Not unless you want to. We will see them all later, I
expect.'

'Later?'

'Well, they are neighbours, after all. There will be

plenty of time to talk with them.' He was guiding her away from the group. They stood looking into the distance, where the hazy outline of Castleview stood against the sky.

'I wonder what castle people could see from there,' Caroline mused out loud.

'It must have been here, on the rising land. A good place for a castle. . .' He looked around at the softly undulating countryside. 'A good place to defend.'

Caroline looked up at him. He had a faraway look on his face. He's probably dreaming of distant hills again, she thought, and sighed.

'Why the sad sigh?' He tucked her hand under his arm.

'Not so sad, really. Just. . . I don't know. . .it seems so unfair. To have a beautiful day like this for a funeral.' She looked across the greening fields. 'I'd rather Terry were alive to see it.'

He remained silent and they began to walk slowly away from the churchyard. He looked again over at the hospital before it was lost to view. 'There are more Terrys, I'm afraid. There will always be more Terrys and tomorrow we go back to them.'

'It never really stops, does it? Patients come and go, but it never really ends.' Caroline was thoughtful.

'No. It might change, but it never finishes. Not this work. That's why we keep at it.' He looked down at the dark head close to his shoulder. 'There are many things that never end.'

She glanced up at him but looked away quickly. His clear blue eyes had the tender look in them that was becoming very familiar.

'Let's sit.' He lowered himself down on a flat stretch of rock and Caroline gingerly joined him. The stone had a faint warmth from the afternoon sun. 'That's a good colour. . .' He was pointing to cheerful yellow wall-flowers swaying in the breeze and wafting their fragrance across the fields.

Caroline smiled. 'Hm. Were you thinking of anything in particular? For that colour, I mean?'

'Well, now that you mention it,' he grinned sheepishly, 'I was rather hoping. . .you don't really dislike it, do you?'

'No.' Caroline smiled. How could she dislike the favourite colour of this yellow-bright man?

'Wouldn't it be all right in a kitchen?' His question sounded so tentative that she laughed lightly. 'Well, wouldn't it?'

'Yes, a yellow kitchen would be lovely.' She coughed with her laughter.

'Really?' Again, he looked so unsure of himself, she wanted to hug him.

'Yes, I definitely think you should have a kitchen full of sunshine.' As she answered, he grinned broadly with obvious relief and she laughed at his expression. 'Have you already bought the paint?'

He nodded and she squeezed his hand. Before she could ask why her opinion was so important, she was distracted by his rising slowly.

'Here comes Tim Mapley.' His voice was low and she turned to see the innkeeper approaching them. His usually kindly face looked drawn and grey, but he attempted to smile as he walked slowly up to them. Caroline stood as she reached out to take his offered hand.

'I just wanted to thank you for the music, Miss Lawson. Terry told me all about the group you started and he would have been right proud.' His voice wavered very slightly as he grasped her hand.

'It was our pleasure, Mr Mapley, all of us. Terry was an important member of the group and we will all miss him a great deal.' She smiled at him. 'We all cared very much about him, and I'm sorry. . .sorry that we couldn't do more. . .' It was difficult to express her feelings to this bereaved man. How did one apologise for failure? She felt that somehow they had failed Terry, but that wouldn't help his father.

'Yes.' He nodded. 'Sometimes all we try to do isn't enough.' He sighed, but attempted another smile. 'Still, it's good to know that he had such friends.'

Impulsively, Caroline held out the 'small pot of blooms. 'Would you like these, Mr Mapley. Please?'

He looked at the large brown eyes filled with sympathy and compassion and took the offered gift. It was good that Dr Hunter had found such a kind girl, he thought. It would be nice to have young folk around. . .'Thank you.' He smiled at Caroline and turned to David.

'Doctor.' Tim held out his hand.

'Tim.' David shook his hand firmly and nodded quietly at him. Caroline watched them enviously. Sometimes men didn't have to say anything to each other; they just seemed to communicate emotions without words.

'We'll be seeing you around then, Doctor.' Tim looked at the young couple standing before him. His statement had a hint of a question as he watched the two young glowing faces. They seemed a natural part of the beginnings of the new spring.

'Yes, Tim, With any luck, we'll be around for quite some time.' David put his arm around Caroline's shoulder lightly and smiled at his new neighbour.

'Aye, that'll be a good thing.' With a short nod, Tim Mapley turned to walk away.

'Do you not have a drive home?' David asked quickly.

A shake of the head was his answer. 'It's a good day for walking. It's not far. . .not far at all.' With a brief wave, Terry's father began the slow walk home with heavy steps.

David and Caroline watched him disappear around the corner of the church and by mutual unspoken consent they began to follow slowly. David kept his arm around her shoulder and Caroline felt the warmth of the sun and his arm. He really is a part of the sun, she thought. She looked up at him and he grinned down at her.

'Did you rehearse the group this week? They were better than they've ever been.' Caroline remembered the glorious singing of the patients.

'It was Bob's idea, of all people.' David laughed lightly. 'The only time that man doesn't twitch is when he's singing.'

She leaned into his warmth. 'It was good to hear you sing again.'

'I had to do some fast sight-reading, I can tell you. Mr Lawrence was actually singing as well, did you notice? I made him learn the bass line and drummed it into him. More of a growl than anything, but at least he was on key!'

Caroline smiled. She had wondered where that rasping deep sound had come from. 'Was Martin singing? I couldn't hear him.'

'No. He just wanted to be there.' They walked slowly and nodded at some of the villagers who were preparing to leave the group at the church steps.

'And where was our Fred?' Caroline still found it hard to be charitable towards the belligerent man. Surely one didn't have to love all the patients. She couldn't really forgive him.

'He stayed behind, with Winston. Poor Fred.' The note of genuine concern in his voice caused Caroline to look up at him. He noticed her glance and answered the unspoken question. 'He's the one who has to live with the consequences of what he did, Caro. That can be a living hell.'

Suddenly Caroline remembered what Dr Staveley had told her. Her mother—she could call her Mother now without effort—had made her husband's life a misery. He had had to live with guilt as well, all his life. He must have had years of suffering, and knowing that was the result of her actions had made her mother retreat into illness.

'I think I can see what you mean.' Caroline spoke thoughtfully and David watched her face closely. She continued in a low voice, 'Living can be more difficult than dying, if one is living with such feelings of guilt. Like my mother.'

David hugged her lightly. 'Yes, Caro. Like your mother.'

'You know about her. . .my mother?' Caroline's eyes shot up to his face and she stopped short.

David took a deep breath. 'Yes, Caro, I know about

your mother.' He dropped his arms to his sides and waited.

'And what else do you know?' Her voice had a dangerous calmness.

'I know what Edward Staveley told you.' David stood calmly, ready to accept her reaction.

Caroline looked down at the ground and bit her lip thoughtfully. 'All of it?'

'I think so.'

Caroline sighed deeply. Slowly she could feel a heavy weight lifting from her. David knew all there was to know. 'When did you talk to him?'

'Before you saw him. He told me what he would tell you. I assume he did. He is a man with a strong sense of honour. He would do whatever he said he was going to do.'

'About my uncle—stepfather—whatever he was?'

'Yes.'

So he had known all this when they had left the hospital. He had known last Sunday when she—— She smiled crookedly up at him. 'Then you must have known what my. . .' she coloured slightly '. . .what I was doing. . .in   your   bedroom. . .'   She   stopped, embarrassed.

David grinned down at her. 'I had an idea. But I wasn't sure you did.' He brushed her cheek with his fingertips. 'Besides, we were both too knackered to be thinking very clearly.'

She lowered her head and kept her eyes at the level of his top jacket button. 'I just wanted. . .to find out. . .' Her words disappeared into her trembling chin.

She felt herself softly enclosed in his strong arms and his whisper was breathing against her ear. 'Your flutters, Caro? You wanted to find out about those flutters of yours?' His lips were brushing her cheek.

She raised her face and met his lips with an aching need. As his mouth deepened with a demanding pressure she moulded her body to fit into the curve of his arms and felt herself being held tightly against his strength.

He lifted his head and tenderly kissed her eyelids, his

mouth roaming over her brow to murmur huskily against her tilted neck, 'And those flutters, my love. . .?'

'Beautiful. . .lovely flutters. . .' She reached under his coat to hold him closer. 'My yellow-bright man, I do love you so much.' She was murmuring against his chest and suddenly her chin was tilted up in a firm grasp and deep blue eyes were scanning her face.

'What did you say?' His voice sounded hoarse and Caroline giggled softly. Why did this man always ask her to repeat things?

She looked up at him, her face glowing with the radiance of her love. 'I said, and you heard me perfectly well, I love you, you yellow-bright person.'

'Yaho-o-o-o-o!' As he let out a loud cheer, David lifted her clear off the ground and swung her around in a high arc. Caroline was breathless.

'Put me down!' She found herself being held high above his shoulders looking down into a laughing face. The man really didn't know his own strength, and what would the villagers say if they saw them now? She tried to wriggle, unsuccessfully, against his firm hold. 'Put me down! Please?'

Slowly he lowered her against his lean body and he just smiled and smiled into her flushed face. Caroline brushed at her wind-blown hair. 'What are you laughing at? You look like a Cheshire cat.' She had to grin at him.

'I'll never stop laughing, my love. Never.' He threatened to whirl her around again and she backed off quickly.

'Oh, no. No more airborne swings, thank you. You'll put your back out.' She brushed at her jacket and kept a wary eye on those muscular arms.

He laughed loudly, 'I certainly don't intend to do that, my love.' He suddenly swung around in a delighted circle and executed a quick jig step on the road. Caroline watched him closely. She wasn't quite sure what he was going to do next. She just hoped no one came along to see this crazy person—this wonderful, crazy, delightful and deeply loved golden person.

David stopped his whirling and stood, breathlessly, still grinning at her. It seemed as if joy and happiness were pouring out of every inch of him. He bowed his head at her, still smiling. 'Ah, my little earth person. . .the sparrow prefers her feet on the ground.' Again his deep laugh floated away on the breeze. 'I will build you a cosy nest, my love, and keep it safe forever.'

He reached out his arms and she eagerly entered into the warm circle and leaned happily on his chest. How could she ever hope to keep up with his energy? But earth people need the sun to live, she thought, and looked up at the fair head gleaming in the afternoon glow. Without his light she would have no warmth or growth or purpose.

As she snuggled happily and listened to the pounding of his heart against her cheek, she heard a noise in the distance and lifted her head. It sounded familiar. She drew back quickly. It was one of the villagers and she made a quick attempt to tidy her hair.

David watched her with a tender smile and shook his head with resignation. He had also seen the slowly approaching car and his smile widened. He gently removed one of the hands trying to return a stray lock of black hair to its rightful place.

'Edward Staveley also said your mother should be well enough in a couple of months to be spending some time outside the hospital.'

Caroline looked up at him. What was he planning now? What else did he know that she didn't? She waited.

He was grinning mischievously. 'Well, we do have two bedrooms.' Caroline nodded. It would be wonderful to have her mother with her, for however brief a time. She felt a strong surge of gratitude to him.

'You have been good to her, David. I am truly grateful. I wouldn't have a mum if it weren't for you.'

He smiled. 'I may have had an ulterior motive, my love. After all, she was the only family of the woman I intended to marry.' He turned his head to watch the approaching car. 'And I'm sure she would like to attend her daughter's wedding.'

'Marry? Wedding?' As the rumble of the rattling engine came alongside them, she didn't believe she had heard him properly. Did he say marry? Her heart seemed to be threatening to burst right out of her.

'Of course.' Keeping one eye on the bouncing car now swaying down the centre of the road, he grabbed her hand. 'Come on, we'd better catch them up while we've got the chance.'

'Who?' She found herself being almost dragged along behind him and she had to run to keep up.

'The vicar. . .that's his car. Hurry up, woman.' He turned his head and laughed. 'You are going to marry me, aren't you?' His eyes seemed to soften under his blowing hair and he slowed down. 'You will, won't you, Caro? I mean. . . I've got all that mushroom paint and three sets of walls to do yet, but. . .'

She stood looking up at the uncertainty she could read in those clear blue eyes that were looking right through to her pounding heart. 'Yes, David. I'll marry you.' Her voice was quiet and she stood on tiptoe to brush his lips as she added softly, 'We have mountains to climb, don't we?'

Throwing back his head, he laughed, with joy. 'We will climb up to the stars and stay there. . .forever and ever! Come on!' Turning to see the old estate wagon going around a bend, he stopped and, putting two fingers to his lips, produced a high, piercing whistle.

DON'T MISS OUT ON HOLIDAY ROMANCE!

Four specially selected brand new novels from popular authors in an attractive easy-to-pack presentation case.

THE TIGER'S LAIR
Helen Bianchin
THE GIRL HE LEFT BEHIND
Emma Goldrick
SPELLBINDING
Charlotte Lamb
FORBIDDEN ATTRACTION
Lilian Peake

This year take your own holiday romance with you.

Look out for the special pack from 29th June, 1990 priced £5.40.

2 COMPELLING READS FOR AUGUST 1990

HONOUR BOUND – Shirley Larson   £2.99

The last time Shelly Armstrong had seen Justin Corbett, she'd been a tongue tied teenager overwhelmed by his good looks and opulent lifestyle. Now she was an accomplished pilot with her own flying school, and equal to Justin in all respects but one – she was still a novice at loving.

SUMMER LIGHTNING – Sandra James   £2.99

The elemental passions of *Spring Thunder* come alive again in the sequel . . .
Maggie Howard is staunchly against the resumption of logging in her small Oregon town – McBride Lumber had played too often with the lives of families there. So when Jared McBride returned determined to reopen the operation, Maggie was equally determined to block his every move – whatever the cost.

W❋RLDWIDE

Zodiac Wordsearch
Competition

How would you like a years supply of Mills & Boon Romances <u>ABSOLUTELY FREE</u>?

Well, you can win them! All you have to do is complete the word puzzle below and send it into us by Dec 31st 1990. The first five correct entries picked out of the bag after this date will each win a years supply of Mills & Boon Romances (Six books every month - worth over £100!) What could be easier?

S	E	C	S	I	P	R	I	A	M	F
I	U	L	C	A	N	C	E	R	L	I
S	A	I	N	I	M	E	G	N	S	R
C	A	P	R	I	C	O	R	N	U	E
S	E	I	R	A	N	G	I	S	I	O
Z	O	D	W	A	T	E	R	B	R	I
O	G	A	H	M	A	T	O	O	A	P
D	R	R	T	O	U	N	I	R	U	R
I	I	B	R	O	R	O	M	G	Q	O
A	V	I	A	N	U	A	N	C	A	C
C	E	L	E	O	S	T	A	R	S	S

Pisces	Aries	Leo	Earth	**Please turn over for entry details**
Cancer	Gemini	Virgo	Star	
Scorpio	Taurus	Fire	Sign	
Aquarius	Libra	Water	Moon	
Capricorn	Sagittarius	Zodiac	Air	

How to enter

All the words listed overleaf, below the word puzzle, are hidden in the grid. You can can find them by reading the letters forwards, backwards, up and down, or diagonally. When you find a word, circle it, or put a line through it. After you have found all the words, the left-over letters will spell a secret message that you can read from left to right, from the top of the puzzle through to the bottom.

Don't forget to fill in your name and address in the space provided and pop this page in an envelope (you don't need a stamp) and post it today.   Competition closes Dec 31st 1990.

Only one entry
per household
(more than one
will render the
entry invalid).

Mills & Boon Competition
Freepost
P.O. Box 236
Croydon
Surrey CR9 9EL

Hidden message _____

_____

Are you a Reader Service subscriber.   Yes ❏   No ❏

Name_____

Address_____

_____

_____

_____ **Postcode**_____

You may be mailed with other offers as a result of entering this competition.
If you would prefer not to be mailed please tick the box. No ❏

COMP9